Andrew Lang, Paul Sylvester

The dead Leman

And other Tales from the French

Andrew Lang, Paul Sylvester

The dead Leman
And other Tales from the French

ISBN/EAN: 9783337073831

Printed in Europe, USA, Canada, Australia, Japan

Cover: Foto ©Andreas Hilbeck / pixelio.de

More available books at **www.hansebooks.com**

THE DEAD LEMAN

AND OTHER TALES FROM THE FRENCH

BY

ANDREW LANG AND PAUL SYLVESTER

LONDON
SWAN SONNENSCHEIN & CO.
PATERNOSTER SQUARE
1889

CONTENTS.

INTRODUCTION.

In England, short stories—tales which may be read in half an hour—are not so popular as they are in France This may perhaps be explained, and certainly it must be regretted. In a brief narrative, or romance, nothing should be wasted, nothing should be superfluous, all should converge rapidly so as to produce the desired effect, or to enhance the interest of the given situation. Hence it is a misfortune that English taste is intolerant of short stories. They are welcomed in a magazine or journal; when collected they are looked on with suspicion. Not long ago a critic in *Blackwood's Magazine* rebuked Mr. Stevenson for publishing a set of *contes* in a volume, as if the performance were almost dishonourable. Some strange prejudice whispers, apparently, that a short story must be a "pot boiler," or at best a rough sketch. Almost the reverse of this theory is often true.

A writer has an idea, say, a set of characters, or a given situation, which ought to be given in some twenty pages. But he is made to understand that he cannot afford thus to waste his idea. If he treats it as it should be treated, he produces a magazine tale which is not very remunerative; and if he were to write a dozen small master-pieces, and reprint them in a volume, he would have, at best, a little praise as the reward of his toil. The result is that the inventor pads and bolsters his idea out into a three-volume novel. He wastes his conception, he dilutes it, he surrounds it with a mob of needless characters, and a world of unnecessary incident; but, at last, he has a three-volume novel before him. It is not, artistically, worth a fraction of what the brief *conte* would have been worth; but it is comparatively prosperous in the commercial sense. So notorious is this, that when an English author has accumulated a budget of brief tales, his publisher often puts them forth in three volumes, under the title of one or other of the narratives. Thus an unwary public may get short stories from Mr. Mudie's without intending it, under the impression that a regular novel has arrived. In this way the art of fiction suffers, the author suffers, and beginners feel obliged to write three volumes of vast and wandering narrative before they have proved, in less laborious fashion, and in a limited field, whether or not they possess the right of telling a story at all.

In France the *conte,* or short story, has always been more fortunate. It is needless, here, to trace the descent of the *conte* from the old *fabliau,* and from the light rhymed tales of La Fontaine. Many circumstances made the short story popular in France. Perhaps the more quick and eager intellect of the people does not dread, as we dread, the effort of awakening the attention afresh a dozen times in one volume. In England we seem to dislike this effort. We prefer to make it only once, to get interested in the characters once for all, and then to loiter with them through, perhaps, 400,000 words of more or less consecutive narrative. If this theory be correct, short stories will never have much success in England, and, consequently, will not often be well written, because there is no prize in praise or money offered to him who writes them well. It would be hard to mention a single collection of *contes* which has really prospered among English-speaking people, except the stories of Poe. Experience proves that the least excellent of Hawthorne's romances is better liked than his volumes of little master-pieces. We seem to hate literary kickshaws, and to clamour for a round of literary beef. Older authors, Fielding and Dickens, at first mixed up brief tales in their long stories, but such tales were felt to be superfluous. Only one of them is immortal, " Wandering Willie's Tale," in *Redgauntlet*, that perfect model of a *conte* in whose narrow range, humour, poetry, the grotesque, the terrible are combined as in no other work of man.

The French short story has for ally the agility of the French mind, which does not decline the labour of awaking its attention afresh at brief intervals. The comparative licence of French art is also favourable to the *conte*. A short story needs a very powerful motive or situation, and the French can use motives and situations, both serious and ludicrous, which the British author must avoid. It is not necessary to discuss here the morality of many *contes* by M. Guy de Maupassant, by "Gyp," by Théo Critt, and half a dozen others. But it is plain to every observer that these writers are permitted to approach sources of mirth, of horror, of pity, of curiosity, which are closed against their English contemporaries. Now the very strength, or if any one prefers it, the very violence of the emotions which the British author has to shun, are congenial to the character of the short story. The *conte* has little room for the links and loops of an English love affair, whether it has to end in marriage or in a broken heart. Adventure, accident, incident, are more appropriate themes, and there are stores of comic or tragic ideas, which we can only read about in the comparative obscurity of a foreign language. The supernatural offers motives well suited to the short story, because in the short story you have not time to become familiar with the strange and the terrible. On the other hand, a ghost who pervades a whole novel, like the White Lady of Avenel, or the spectre in the *Wizard's Son*, ceases to alarm or greatly to interest.

We *may* use the supernatural in English, and our tales which deal with it—*Wandering Willie, Thrawn Janet, The Beleaguered City*—are perhaps better than anything of the kind in French. It would be difficult to name a good ghost story in French, though George Sand has a delicate touch in the supernatural. In spite of our advantage here, it is curious that Poe, the master of the *conte* in English, never introduces the supernatural as an agent in his plots.

It is not probable that the stories in this little collection will win many English readers to an affection for the *conte*, though the translators hope against hope for this result. There are, apparently, people in this highly over-educated realm of England who prefer to read French stories in English. To them, if they care to leave their translations of M. Fortuné du Boisgobey and M. Zola, these versions of tales more or less representative and classic are respectfully offered. They are chosen from various authors well known to fame, and it is curious that, in one respect, they lack variety. The motive is usually terrible and tragic, probably because, as we have said, the short story needs powerful and striking situations. Comic situations will also do, of course, but here the difference between the French and the English literary taste for jokes comes in. The anecdotes which we and the Americans "swap" in conversation, the "good stories" of oral tradition, and of smoking rooms, are worked over by the French with literary skill. But then they are "gentlemen's stories," as one of Thackeray's ladies says, and shall not by us be introduced to our audience, when the British matron may be present.

A few words may be said about the tales of which we offer versions. *The Dead Leman* is from *La Morte Amoureuse* of Théophile Gautier. Very probably this is one of the tales concerning which he told MM. de Goncourt that he often began them in verse, but was forced after all, by the public hatred of poetry, to tell them in prose. It is rather a poetic impression, than a sense of spiritual dread, (like that which haunts readers of Mr. Stevenson's *Thrawn Janet*,) that Gautier meant to produce. The two real elements of his genius, as he said himself, were wild buffoonery and deep melancholy. He might have added, a singular love of things rich, bright, coloured, and luxurious, — of gold, and roses, and ivory,—and a rare skill in painting them with epithets. Examples of this are common in *La Morte Amoureuse*. Had the tale been successful enough, he would have been accused by spiteful smatterers of stealing it from the famous and terrible Greek ghost story which opens the book of Phlegon, *De Mirabilibus*. But Phlegon's tale of the Dead Bride is told with the "realism" of De Foe, and a person with a taste for ghosts may shudder as he reads Gautier scarcely aims at this result. From Balzac we have only taken "The Doctor's Story," *La Grande Brétêche*. As this version may fall into the hands of a reader who does not know the plot, it is only possible to hint at its resemblances to one of Poe's best-known tales.

From Mérimée we take the spirited story of the "Capture of the Redoubt," and "The Etruscan Vase," chiefly because in the hero Mérimée sketched himself, at least if M. de Goncourt's report is correct.[1]

"They tell me that Mérimée is a thing wholly

---

[1] *Journal*, Jan. 3, 1864.

compact of the fear of ridicule, which fell out thus: When he was a child, he was scolded one day, and as he left the room he heard his father and mother laugh at his dolorous face.

"He swore that he would never be laughed at again; he kept his word, and he dried up in the process."

Saint Clair did not wholly "dry up" in "The Etruscan Vase," and probably Mérimée, when he wrote the tale, was protesting in his own favour.

"These Lots to be Sold," is a fair example of About's lighter manner, and "A Conversion" is a specimen of the lady's work who calls herself Th. Bentzon.

Perhaps a few words should be said on translation. Some arts have been lost; the art of translation has never been discovered. All translators labour after it; we seek it like hidden treasure; we never find it. You cannot pour the wine without spilling "from the golden cup to the silver." Plenty of the original vintage has been spilt in these attempts to pour it forth; the English language will not reply in tune to the touch of the French. Perhaps this is most obvious in *The*

Dead Leman, because the faint archaism, the perfume, the poetry of Gautier's prose is the most difficult to reproduce. An American attempt has been made. We refrain from quoting this essay, in which Romuald does not go to bed, but "retires," and in which nothing begins, but everything "commences." The great and good-humoured shade of Théophile will pardon the vain efforts of his alien admirers.

A. L.
P. S.

THE DEAD LEMAN.

(THÉOPHILE GAUTIER.)

HAVE I ever loved, you ask me, my brother? Yes, I have loved! The story is dread and marvellous, and, for all my threescore years, I scarce dare stir the ashes of that memory. To you I can refuse nothing; to a heart less steeled than yours this tale could never be told by me. For these things were so strange that I can scarce believe they came into my own existence. Three long years was I the puppet of a delusion of the devil. Three long years was I a parish priest by day, while by night, in dreams (God grant they were but dreams!), I

B

led the life of a child of this world, of a lost soul! For one kind glance at a woman's face was my spirit to be doomed; but at length, with God to aid and my patron saint, it was given to me to drive away the evil spirit that possessed me.

I lived a double life, by night and by day. All day long was I a pure priest of the Lord, concerned only with prayer and holy things; but no sooner did I close my eyes in sleep than I was a young knight, a lover of women, of horses, of hounds, a drinker, a dicer, a blasphemer, and, when I woke at dawn, meseemed that I was fallen on sleep, and did but dream that I was a priest. From those years of dreaming certain memories yet remain with me; memories of words and things that will not down. Ay, though I have never left the walls of my vicarage, he who heard me would rather deem me one that had lived in the world and left it, to die in religion, and end in the breast of God his tumultuous days, than for a priest grown old in a forgotten cure, deep in a wood, and far from the things of this earth.

Yes, I have loved as never man loved, with a wild love and a terrible, so that I marvel my heart did not burst in twain. Oh, the nights of long ago!

From my earliest childhood had I felt the call to be a priest. This was the end of all my studies, and, till I was twenty-four, my days were one long training. My theological course achieved, I took the lesser orders, and at length, at the end of Holy Week, was to be the hour of my ordination.

I had never entered the world; *my* world was the college close. Vaguely I knew that woman existed, but of women I never thought. My heart was wholly pure. Even my old and infirm mother I saw but twice a year; of other worldly relations I had none.

I had no regrets, and no hesitations in taking the irrevocable vow; nay, I was full of an impatient joy. Never did a young bridegroom so eagerly count the hours to his wedding. In my broken sleep I dreamed of saying the Mass. To be a priest seemed to me the noblest thing in the world, and I would have disdained the estate of poet or of king. To be a priest! My ambition saw nothing higher.

All this I tell you that you may know how little I deserved that which befel me; that you may know how inexplicable was the fascination by which I was overcome.

The great day came, and I walked to church as if I were winged or trod on air. I felt an angelic beatitude, and marvelled at the gloomy and thoughtful faces of my companions, for we were many. The night I had passed in prayer. I was all but entranced in ecstasy. The bishop, a venerable old man, was in my eyes like God the Father bowed above His own eternity, and I seemed to see heaven open beyond the arches of the minster.

You know the ceremony: the Benediction, the Communion in both kinds, the anointing of the palms of the hands with consecrated oil, and finally the celebration of the Holy Rite, offered up in company with the bishop. On these things I will not linger, but oh, how true is the word of Job, that he is foolish who maketh not a covenant with his eyes! I chanced to raise my head, and saw before me, so near that it seemed I could touch her, though in reality she was at some distance, and on the farther side of a railing, a young dame royally clad, and of incomparable beauty.

It was as if scales had fallen from my eyes; and I felt like a blind man who suddenly recovers his sight. The bishop, so splendid a moment ago, seemed to fade; through all the church was darkness, and the candles paled in their sconces of gold, like stars at dawn. Against the gloom that lovely thing shone out like a heavenly revelation, seeming herself to be the fountain of light, and to give it rather than receive it. I cast down my eyes, vowing that I would not raise them again; my attention was failing, and I scarce knew what I did. The moment afterwards, I opened my eyes, for through my eyelids I saw her glittering in a bright penumbra, as when one has stared at the sun. Ah, how beautiful she was! The greatest painters, when they have sought in heaven for ideal beauty, and have brought to earth the portrait of our Lady, come never near the glory of this vision! Pen of poet, or palette of painter, can give no idea of her. She was tall, with the carriage of a goddess; her fair hair flowed about her brows in rivers of gold. Like a crowned queen she stood there, with her broad white brow, and dark eyebrows; with her eyes that had the brightness and life of the green sea, and at one glance made or marred the destiny of a man. They were astonishingly clear and brilliant, shooting rays like arrows, which I could actually see winging straight for my heart. I know not if the flame that lighted them came from heaven or hell, but from one or other assuredly it came. Angel or devil, or both; this woman was no child of Eve, the mother of us all. White teeth shone in her smile, little dimples came and went with each movement of her mouth, among the roses of her cheeks. There was a lustre as of agate on the smooth and shining skin of her half-clad shoulders, and chains of great pearls no whiter than her neck fell over her breast. From time to time she lifted her head in snake-like motion, and set the silvery ruffles of her raiment quivering. She wore a flame-coloured velvet robe, and from the ermine lining of her sleeves her delicate hands came and went, as transparent as the fingers of the dawn. As I gazed at her, I felt within me, as it were, the opening of gates that had ever been barred; I saw sudden vistas of an unknown future; all life seemed altered, new thoughts wakened in my heart. A horrible pain took possession of me; each minute seemed at once a moment and an age. The ceremony went on and on, and I was being carried far from the world, at whose gates my new desires were beating. I said "Yes" when I wished to say "No," when my whole soul protested against the words my tongue was uttering. A hidden force seemed to drag them from me. This it is perhaps which makes so many young girls walk to the altar with the firm resolve to refuse the husband who is forced on them, and this is why not one of them does what she intends. This is why so many poor novices take the veil, though they are determined to tear it into shreds, rather than pronounce the vows. None dares cause so great a scandal before so many observers, nor thus betray such general expectation. The will of all imposes itself on you; the gaze of all weighs upon you like a cope of lead. And, again, all is so clearly arranged in advance, so evidently irrevocable, that the intention of refusal is crushed, and disappears.

The expression of the unknown beauty changed as the ceremony advanced. Tender and caressing at first, it became contemptuous and disdainful. With an effort that might have moved a mountain, I strove to cry out that I would never be a priest; it was in vain, my tongue clave to the roof of my mouth, I could not refuse even by a sign. Though wide-awake, I seemed to be in one of those night-mares, wherein for your life you cannot utter the word on which your life depends. She appeared to understand the torture which I endured, and cast on me a glance of divine pity and divine promise. "Be mine," she seemed to say, "and I shall make thee happier than God and heaven, and His angels will be jealous of thee. Tear that shroud of death wherein thou art swathed, for I am beauty, and I am youth, and I am life; come to me and we shall be love. What can Jehovah offer thee in exchange for thy youth? Our life will flow like a dream in the eternity of a kiss. Spill but the wine from that chalice, and thou art free, and I will carry thee to the unknown isles, and thou shalt sleep on my breast in a bed of gold beneath a canopy of silver, for I love thee and would fain take thee from thy God, before whom so many noble hearts pour forth the incense of their love, which dies before it reaches the heaven where He dwells." These words I seemed to hear singing in the sweetest of tunes, for there was a music in her look, and the words which her eyes sent to me resounded in my heart as if they had been whispered in my soul. I was ready to foreswear God, and yet I went duly through each rite of the ceremony. She cast me a second glance, so full of entreaty and despair, that I felt more swords pierce my breast than stabbed the heart of our Lady of Sorrows.

It was over, and I was a priest.

Then never did human face declare so keen a sorrow: the girl who sees her betrothed fall dead at her side, the mother by the empty cradle of her child, Eve at the gate of Paradise, the miser who seeks his treasure and finds a stone, even they look less sorely smitten, less inconsolable.

The blood left her fair face pale, white as marble she seemed; her lovely arms fell powerless, her feet failed beneath her, and she leaned against a pillar of the church. For me, I staggered to the door, with a white, wet face, breathless, with all the weight of all the dome upon my head. As I was crossing the threshold, a hand seized mine, a woman's hand. I had never felt before a woman's hand in mine. It was cold as the skin of a serpent, yet it burned me like a brand. "Miserable man, what hast thou done?" she whispered, and was lost in the crowd.

The old bishop paused, and gazed severely at me, who was a piteous spectacle, now red, now pale, giddy and faint. One of my fellows had compassion on me, and led me home. I could not have found the way alone. At the corner of a street, while the young priest's head was turned, a black page, strangely clad, came up to me, and gave me, as he passed, a little leathern case, with corners of wrought gold, signing to me to hide it. I thrust it into my sleeve, and there kept it till I was alone in my cell. Then I opened the clasp; there were but these words written : " Clarimonde, at the Palazzo Concini." So little of a worldling was I, that I had never heard of Clarimonde, despite her fame, nay, nor knew where the Palazzo Concini might be. I made a myriad guesses, each wilder than the other; but truth to tell, so I did but see her again, I recked little whether Clarimonde were a noble lady, or no better than one of the wicked.

This love, thus born in an hour, had struck root too deep for me to dream of casting it from my heart. This woman had made me utterly her own, a glance had been enough to change me, her will had passed upon me; I lived not for myself, but in her and for her.

Many mad things did I, kissing my hand where hers had touched it, repeating her name for hours;—

Clarimonde, Clarimonde! I had but to close my eyes, and I saw her as distinctly as if she had been present. Then I murmured to myself the words that beneath the church porch she had spoken: "Miserable man, what hast thou done?" I felt all the horror of that strait wherein I was, and the dead and terrible aspect of the life that I had chosen was now revealed. To be a priest! Never to love, to know not youth nor sex, to turn away from beauty, to close the eyes, to crawl in the chill shade of a cloister or a church; to see none but deathly men, to watch by the nameless corpses of folk unknown, to wear a cassock like my own mourning for myself, my own raiment for my coffin's pall!

Then life arose in me like a lake in flood, my blood coursed in my veins, my youth burst forth in a moment; like the aloe, which flowers but once in a hundred years, and breaks into blossom with a sound of thunder!

How was I again to have sight of Clarimonde?

I had no excuse for leaving the seminary, for I knew nobody in the town, and indeed was only waiting there till I should be appointed to my parish. I tried to remove the bars of the window, but to descend without a ladder was impossible. Then, again, I could only escape by night, when I should be lost in the labyrinth of streets. These difficulties, which would have been nothing to others, were enormous to a poor priest like me, now first fallen in love, without experience, or money, or knowledge of the world.

Ah, had I not been a priest I might have seen her every day, I might have been her lover, her husband, I said to myself in the blindness of my heart. In place of being swathed in a cassock I might have worn silk and velvet, chains of gold, a sword and feather like all the fair young knights. My locks would not be tonsured, but would fall in perfumed curls about my neck. But one hour spent before an altar, and some gabbled words, had cut me off from the company of the living. With my own hand I had sealed the stone upon my tomb, and turned the key in the lock of my prison!

I walked to the window. The sky was heavenly blue, the trees had clothed them in the raiment of spring, all nature smiled with mockery in her smile. The square was full of people coming and going: young exquisites, young beauties, two by two, were walking in the direction of the gardens. Workmen sang drinking songs as they passed; on all sides were a life, a movement, a gaiety that did but increase my sorrow and my solitude. A young mother, on the steps of the gate, was playing with her child, kissing its little rosy mouth, with a thousand of the caresses, the childlike and the divine caresses that are the secret of mothers. Hard by the father, with folded arms above a happy heart, smiled sweetly as he watched them. I could not endure the sight. I shut the window, and threw myself on the bed in a horrible jealousy and hatred, so that I gnawed my fingers and my coverlet like a starved wild beast.

How many days I lay thus I know not, but at last, as I turned in a spasm of rage, I saw the Abbé Sérapion curiously considering me. I bowed my head in shame, and hid my face with my hands.

"Romuald, my friend," said he, "some strange thing hath befallen thee. Satan hath desired to have thee, that he may sift thee like wheat; he goeth about thee to devour thee as a raging lion. Beware and make thyself a breastplate of prayer, a shield of the mortifying of the flesh. Fight, and thou shalt overcome. Be not afraid with any discouragement, for the firmest hearts and the most surely guarded have known hours like these. Pray, fast, meditate, and the evil spirit will pass away from thee."

Then Sérapion told me that the priest of C—— was dead, that the bishop had appointed me to this charge, and that I must be ready by the morrow. I nodded assent, and the Abbé departed. I opened my missal and strove to read in it, but the lines waved confusedly, and the volume slipped unheeded from my hands.

Next day Sérapion came for me; two mules were waiting for us at the gate with our slender baggage, and we mounted as well as we might. As we traversed the streets I looked for Clarimonde, in each balcony, at every window; but it was too early, and the city was yet asleep. When we had passed the gates, and were climbing the height, I turned back for a last glance at the place that was the home of Clarimonde. The shadow of a cloud lay on the city, the red roofs and the blue were mingled in a mist, whence rose here and there white puffs of smoke. By some strange optical effect, one house stood up, golden in a ray of light, far above the roofs that were mingled in the mist. A league away though it was, it seemed quite close to us—all was plain to see, turrets, balconies, parapets, the very weather-cocks.

"What is that palace we see yonder in the sunlight?" said I to Sérapion.

He shaded his eyes with his hand, looked, and answered,—

"That is the old palace which Prince Concini has given to Clarimonde the harlot. Therein dreadful things are done."

Even at that moment, whether it were real or a vision I know not now, methought I saw a white and slender shape cross the terrace, glance, and disappear. It was Clarimonde!

Ah, did she know how in that hour, at the height of the rugged way which led me from her, even at the crest of the path I should never tread again, I was watching her, eager and restless, watching the palace where she dwelt, and which a freak of light and shadow seemed to bring near me, as if inviting me to enter and be lord of all? Doubtless she knew it, so closely bound was her heart to mine; and this it was which had urged her, in the raiment of the night, to climb the palace terrace in the frosty dews of dawn.

The shadow slipped over the palace, and, anon, there was but a motionless sea of roofs, marked merely by a billowy undulation of forms. Sérapion pricked on his mule, mine also quickened, and a winding of the road hid from me for ever the city of S., where I was to return no more. At the end of three days' journey through melancholy fields, we saw the weather-cock of my parish church peeping above the trees. Some winding lanes, bordered by cottages and gardens, brought us to the building, which was of no great splendour. A porch with a few mouldings, and two or three pillars rudely carved in sandstone, a tiled roof with counterforts of the same stone as the pillars,—that was all. To the left was the graveyard, deep in tall grasses, with an iron cross in the centre. The priest's house was to the right, in the shadow of the church. Simplicity could not be more simple, nor cleanliness less lovely. Some chickens were pecking at a few grains of oats on the ground as we entered. The sight of a priest's frock seemed too familiar to alarm them, and they scarcely moved to let us pass. Then we heard a hoarse and wheezy bark, and an old dog ran up to greet us. He was the dog of the late priest—dim-eyed, grey, with every sign of a dog's extreme old age. I patted him gently, and he walked along by my side with an air of inexpressible satisfaction. An elderly woman, my predecessor's house-keeper, came in her turn to greet us; and when she learned that I meant to keep her in my service, to keep the dog and the chickens, with all the furniture that her master had left her at his death—above all, when the Abbé Sérapion paid what she asked on the spot—her joy knew no bounds.

When I had been duly installed, Sérapion returned

to the college, and I was left alone. Unsupported, uncomforted as I was, the thought of Clarimonde again beset me, nor could I drive her memory away for all my efforts. One evening, as I walked among the box-lined paths of my little garden, I fancied that I saw among the trees the form of a woman, who followed all my movements, and whose green eyes glistened through the leaves. Green as the sea shone her eyes, but it was no more than a vision, for when I crossed to the other side of the alley, nothing did I find but the print of a little foot on the sand—a foot like the foot of a child. Now the garden was girt with high walls, and, for all my search, I could find no living thing within them. I have never been able to explain this incident, which, after all, was nothing to the strange adventures that were to follow.

Thus did I live for a whole year, fulfilling every duty of the priesthood,—preaching, praying, fasting, visiting the sick, denying myself necessaries that

I might give to the poor. But within me all was dry and barren,—the fountains of grace were sealed. I knew not the happiness which goes with the consciousness of a holy mission fulfilled. My heart was otherwhere; the words of Clarimonde dwelt on my lips like the ballad burden a man repeats against his will. Oh, my brother, consider this! For the lifting up of mine eyes to behold a woman have I been harried these many years, and my life hath been troubled for ever.

I shall not hold you longer with the story of these defeats and these victories, and the fresh defeats of my soul; let me come to the beginning of the new life.

One night there was a violent knocking at my gate. The old housekeeper went to open it, and the appearance of a man richly clad in an out-landish fashion, tawny of hue, armed with a long dagger, stood before her in the light of her lantern. She was terrified, but he soothed her, saying that he needs must see me instantly concerning a matter of my ministry. Barbara brought him upstairs to the room where I was about going to bed. There the man told me that his mistress, a lady of high degree, was on the point of death, and desired to see a priest. I answered that I was ready to follow him, and taking with me such matters as are needful for extreme unction, I went down hastily. At the door were two horses, black as night, their breath rising in white clouds of vapour. The man held my stirrup while I mounted; then he laid one hand on the pommel, and vaulted on the other horse. Gripping his beast with his knees, he gave him his head, and we started with the speed of an arrow, my horse keeping pace with his own. We seemed in running to devour the way; the earth flitted grey beneath us, the black trees fled in the darkness like an army in rout. A forest we crossed, so gloomy and so frozen cold that I felt in all my veins a shudder of superstitious dread. The sparks struck from the flints by our coursers' feet followed after us like a trail of fire, and whoever saw us must have deemed us two ghosts riding the nightmare. Will-o'-the-wisps glittered across our path, the night birds clamoured in the forest deeps, and now and again shone out the burning eyes of wild cats.

The manes of the horses tossed more wildly on the wind, the sweat ran down their sides, their breath came thick and loud. But whenever they slackened the groom called on them with a cry like nothing that ever came from a human throat, and again they ran their furious course. At last the tempest of their flight reached its goal; suddenly there stood before us a great dark mass, with shining points of flame. Our horses' hoofs clattered louder on a drawbridge, and we thundered through the dark depths of a vaulted entrance which gaped between two monstrous towers. Within the castle all was confusion,—servants with burning torches ran hither and thither through the courts, on the staircases lights rose and fell. I beheld a medley of vast buildings, columns, arches, parapet and balcony,—a bewildering world of royal or of fairy palaces. The negro page who had given me the tablets of Clarimonde, and whom I recognised at a glance, helped me to alight. A seneschal in black velvet, with a golden chain about his neck, and an ivory wand in his hand, came forward to meet me, great tears rolling down his cheeks to his snowy beard.

"Too late," he said; "too late, sir priest! But if thou hast not come in time to save the soul, watch, I pray thee, with the unhappy body of the dead."

He took me by the arm; he led me to the hall, where the corpse was lying, and I wept as bitterly as he, deeming that the dead was Clarimonde, the well and wildly loved. There stood a *prie-dieu* by the bed: a blue flame flickering from a cup of bronze cast all about the chamber a doubtful light, and here and there set the shadows fluttering.

In a chiselled vase on the table was one white rose faded, a single petal clinging to the stem; the rest had fallen like fragrant tears and lay beside the vase. A broken black mask, a fan, masquerading gear of every kind were huddled on the chairs, and showed that death had come, unlooked for and unheralded, to that splendid house. Not daring to cast mine eyes upon the bed, I kneeled, and fervently began to repeat the Psalms, thanking God that between this woman and me He had set the tomb, so that now her name might come like a thing enskied and sainted in my prayers.

By degrees this ardour slackened, and I fell a-dreaming. This chamber, after all, had none of the air of a chamber of death. In place of the fetid, corpse-laden atmosphere that I was wont to breathe in these vigils, there floated gently through the warmth a vapour of orient essences, a perfume of woman and of love. The pale glimmer of the lamp seemed rather the twilight of pleasure, than the yellow burning of the taper that watches by the dead. I began to think of the rare hazard that brought me to Clarimonde in the moment when I had lost her for ever, and a sigh came from my breast. Then meseemed that one answered with a sigh behind me, and I turned unconsciously. 'Twas but an echo, but, as I turned, mine eyes fell on that which they had shunned—the bed where Clarimonde lay in state. The flowered and crimson curtains, bound up with loops of gold, left the dead woman plain to view, lying at her length, with hands folded on her breast. She was covered with a linen veil, very white and glistering, the more by reason of the dark purple hangings, and so fine was the shroud that her fair body shone through it, with those beautiful soft waving lines, as of the swan's neck, that not even death could harden. Fair she was as a statue of alabaster carved by some skilled man for the tomb of a queen; fair as a young maid asleep beneath new-fallen snow.

I could endure no longer. The air as of a bower of love, the scent of the faded rose intoxicated me, and I strode through the chamber, stopping at each turn to gaze at the beautiful dead beneath the transparent shroud. Strange thoughts haunted my brain. I fancied that she was not really gone, that it was but a device to draw me within her castle gates, and to tell me all her love. Nay, one moment methought I saw her foot stir beneath its white swathings, and break the stiff lines of the shroud.

"Is she really Clarimonde?" I asked myself presently. "What proof have I? The black page may have entered the household of some other lady. Mad must I be thus to disquiet myself."

But the beating of my own heart answered me, "It is she! It is she!"

I drew near the bed, and looked with fresh attention at that which thus perplexed me. Shall I confess it? The perfection of her beauty, though shadowed and sanctified by death, troubled my heart, and that long rest of hers was wondrous like a living woman's sleep. I forgot that I had come there to watch by a corpse, and I dreamed that I was a young bridegroom on the threshold of the chamber of the veiled, half-hidden bride. Broken with sorrow, wild with joy, shuddering with dread and desire, I stooped toward the dead and raised a corner of the sheet. Gently I raised it, holding my breath as though I feared to waken her. My blood coursed so vehemently that I heard it rushing and surging through the veins of my temples. My brow was dank with drops of sweat, as if I had lifted no film of linen, but a weighty grave-stone of marble.

There lay Clarimonde, even as I had seen her on the day of mine ordination; even so delightful was she, and death in Clarimonde seemed but a wilful charm. The pallor of her cheeks, her dead lips' fading rose, her long downcast eyelids, with their brown lashes breaking the marble of her cheek, all gave her an air of melancholy, and of purity, of pensive patience that had an inexpressible winning magic. Her long loose hair, the small blue flowers yet scattered through it, pillowed her head, and veiled the splendour of her shoulders. Her fair hands, clear and pure as the consecrated wafer, were crossed in an attitude of holy rest and silent prayer, that suffered not the exquisite roundness and ivory polish of her pearled arms to prove, even in death, too triumphant a lure of men.

Long did I wait and watch her silently, and still the more I gazed, the less I could deem that life had left for ever her beautiful body. I knew not if it were an illusion, or a reflection from the lamp, but it was as if the blood began to flow again beneath that dead white of her flesh, and yet she lay eternally, immovably still. I touched her arm; it was cold, but no colder than her hand had been on the day when it met mine beneath the church porch.

I fell into my old attitude, stooping my face above her face, while down upon her rained the warm dew of my tears. Oh bitterness of impotence and of despair, oh wild agony of that death watch!

The night crept on, and as I felt that the eternal separation drew near, I could not deny myself the sad last delight of one kiss on the dead lips that held all my love.

Oh, miracle! A light breath mingled with my breath, and the mouth of Clarimonde answered to the touch of mine! Her eyes opened, and softly shone. She sighed, she uncrossed her arms, and folding them about my neck in a ravished ecstasy.

"Ah, Romuald, it is thou!" she said, in a voice as sweet and languishing as the last tremblings of a lyre. "Ah, Romuald, what makest thou here? So long have I waited for thee that I am dead. Yet now we are betrothed, now I may see thee, and visit thee. Farewell, Romuald, farewell! I love thee. It is all that I had to tell thee, and I give thee again that life which thou gavest me with thy kiss. Soon shall we meet again."

Her head sank down, but still her arms clung to me as if they would hold me for ever. A wild gust of wind burst open the window and broke into the room. The last leaf of the white rose fluttered like a bird's wing on the stem, and then fell and flew through the open casement, bearing with it the soul of Clarimonde.

The lamp went out, and I fell fainting on the breast of the beautiful corpse.

When I came to myself I was lying on my own bed in the little chamber of the priest's house; my hand had slipped from beneath the coverlet, the old dog was licking it. Barbara hobbled and trembled about the room, opening and shutting drawers, and shaking powders into glasses. The old woman gave a cry of delight when she saw me open my eyes. The dog yelped and wagged his tail, but I was too weak to utter a word or make the slightest movement. Later, I learned that for three days I had lain thus, with no sign of life but a scarce perceptible breathing. These three days do not count in my life; I know not where my spirit went wandering all that time, whereof I keep not the slightest memory. Barbara told me that the same bronzed man who had come for me at night, brought me back in a closed litter next morning and instantly went his way. So soon as I could recall my thoughts, I reviewed each incident of that fatal night. At first I deemed that I had been duped by art magic, but presently actual, palpable circumstances destroyed that belief. I could not suppose that I had been dreaming, for Barbara, no less than myself, had seen the man with the two coal-black steeds, and she described them accurately. Yet no one knew of any castle in the neighbourhood at all like that in which I had found Clarimonde again.

One morning Sérapion entered my room ; he had come with all haste in answer to Barbara's message about my illness. Though this declared his affection for me, none the more did his visit give me pleasure. There was somewhat inquisitive and piercing, to my mind, in the very glance of Sérapion, and I felt like a criminal in his presence. He it was who first discovered my secret disquiet, and I bore him a grudge for being so clear-sighted.

While he was asking about my health in accents of honeyed hypocrisy, his eyes, as yellow as a lion's, were sounding the depths of my soul. Presently,—

"The famous harlot Clarimonde is dead," says he, in a piercing tone,—"dead at the close of an eight days' revel. It was a feast of Belshazzar or of Cleopatra. Good God, what an age is ours! The guests were served by dusky slaves who spoke no tongue known among men, and who seemed like spirits from the pit. The livery of the least of them might have beseemed an emperor on a coronation day. Wild tales are told of this same Clarimonde, and all her loves have perished miserably or by violence. They say she was a ghost, a female vampire, but I believe she was the devil himself."

He paused, watching me, who could not master a sudden movement at the name of Clarimonde.

"Satan's claw is long," said Sérapion, with a stern glance, "and tombs ere now have given up their dead. Threefold should be the seal upon the grave of Clarimonde, for this is not, men say, the first time she hath died. God be with thee, Romuald!"

So speaking, Sérapion departed with slow steps, and I saw him no more as at that time.

Time passed, and I was well again. Nay, I deemed that the fears of Sérapion and my own terrors were too great, till, one night, I dreamed a dream.

Scarce had I tasted the first drops of the cup of sleep, when I heard the curtains of my bed open and the rings rang. I raised myself suddenly on my arm, and saw the shadow of a woman standing by me.

Straightway I knew her for Clarimonde.

She held in her hand a little lamp, such as is placed in tombs, and the light touched her slim fingers to a rosy hue, that faded away in the milk-white of her arms. She was clad on with naught but the linen shroud that veiled her when she lay in state; the folds were clasped about her breast, as it were in pudency, by a hand all too small. So white she was that her shroud and her body were blended in the pallid glow of the lamp.

Swathed thus in the fine tissue that betrayed every line of her figure, she seemed a marble image of some lady at the bath rather than a living woman. Dead or living, statue or woman, spirit or flesh, her beauty was ever the same, only the glitter of her sea-green eye was dulled,—only the mouth, so red of old, wore but a tender tint of rose, like the white rose of her cheeks. The little blue flowers that I had seen in her hair were sere now, and all but bloomless; yet so winning was she, so winning that, despite the strangeness of the adventure, and her inexplicable invasion of my chamber, I was not afraid for one moment.

She placed the lamp on the table, and sat down by my bed-foot. Then, in those soft and silver accents which I never heard from any lips but hers,—

"Long have I made thee wait for me," she said, "and thou must have deemed that I had forgotten thee quite. But lo! I come from far, very far,—even from that land whence no traveller has returned. There is no sunlight nor moon in the country whence I wander, only shadow and space. There the foot finds no rest, nor the wandering wing any way; yet here am I, behold me, for Love can conquer Death. Ah, what sad faces and terrible eyes have I seen in my voyaging, and in what labour hath my soul been to find my body and to make her home therein again! How hard to lift was the stone that they had laid on me for a covering! Lo, my hands are sorely wounded in that toil! Kiss them, my love, and heal them." And she laid her chill palms on my mouth, that I kissed many times, she smiling on me with an inexpressible sweetness of delight.

To my shame be it spoken, I had wholly forgotten the counsels of the Abbé Sérapion, and the sacred character of my ministry. I fell unresisting at the first attack. Nay, I did not even try to bid the tempter avaunt, but succumbed without a struggle before the sweet freshness of Clarimonde's fair body. Poor child! for all that is come and gone, I can scarce believe that she was indeed a devil; surely there was naught of the devil in her aspect. Never hath Satan better concealed his claws and his horns!

She was crouching on the side of my bed, her heels drawn up beneath her in an attitude of careless and provoking grace. Once and again she would pass her little hands among my locks, and curl them, as if to try what style best suited my face. It is worth noting that I felt no astonishment at an adventure so marvellous,—nay, as in a dream the strangest events fail to surprise us, even so the whole encounter seemed to me perfectly natural.

"I loved thee long before I saw thee, Romuald, my love, and I sought for thee everywhere. Thou wert my dream, and I beheld thee in the church at that fatal hour. 'It is he,' I whispered to myself, and cast on thee a glance fulfilled of all the love wherewith I had loved, and did love, and shall love thee; a glance that would have ruined the soul of a cardinal, or brought a king with all his court to my feet.

"But thou wert not moved, and before my love thou didst place the love of God.

"Ah, 'tis of God that I am jealous,—God

whom thou hast loved and lovest more than we.

"Miserable woman that I am! Never shall I have all thy heart for myself alone,—for me, whom thou didst awaken with one kiss; for me, Clarimonde the dead; for me, who for thy sake have broken the portals of the grave, and am come to offer to thee a life that hath been taken up again for this one end to make thee happy."

So she spoke; and every word was broken in on by maddening caresses, till my brain swam, and I feared not to console her by this awful blasphemy, namely,—

That my love of her passed my love of God!

Then the fire of her eyes was rekindled, and they blazed as it had been the chrysoprase stone.

"Verily thou lovest me with a love like thy love of God," she cried, making her fair arms a girdle for my body. "Then thou shalt come with me, and whithersoever I go there wilt thou follow. Thou wilt leave thine ugly black robes, thou wilt be of all knights the proudest and the most envied. The acknowledged lover of Clarimonde shalt thou be, of her who refused a Pope! Ah, happy life, ah, golden days that shall be ours! When do we mount and ride, *mon gentilhomme?*"

"To-morrow," I cried in my madness.

"To-morrow," she answered. "I shall have time to change this robe of mine that is somewhat scant, nor fit for voyaging. Also must I speak with my retainers, that think me dead in good earnest, and lament me as well as they may. Money, carriages, change of raiment, all shall be ready for thee; at this hour to-morrow will I seek thee. Good-bye, sweetheart." -

She touched my brow with her lips, the lamp faded into darkness, the curtains closed, a sleep like lead came down on me, sleep without a dream.

I wakened late, troubled by the memory of my dream, which at length I made myself believe was but a vision of the night. Yet it was not without dread that I sought rest again, praying Heaven to guard the purity of my slumber.

Anon I fell again into a deep sleep, and my dream began again. The curtains opened, and there stood Clarimonde, not pale in her pale shroud, nor with the violets of death upon her cheek; but gay, bright, splendid, in a travelling robe of green velvet with trappings of gold, and kilted up on one side to show a satin undercoat. Her fair, curled locks fell in great masses from under a large black beaver hat, with strange white plumes; in her hand she held a little riding-whip, topped with a golden whistle. With this she touched me gently, saying,—

"Awake, fair sleeper! Is it thus you prepare for your voyage? I had thought to find you alert. Rise, rise quickly; we have no time to lose!"

I leaped out of bed.

"Come, dress, and let us be gone," she said,

showing me a little packet she had brought. " Our horses are fretting and champing at the gate. We should be ten leagues from here."

I arrayed myself in haste, while she instructed me, handed me the various articles of a knight's attire, and laughed at my clumsiness. She dressed my hair, and when all was done, gave me a little Venice pocket mirror in a silver frame, crying,—

" What think you of yourself now? Will you take me for your *valet de chambre?*"

I did not know my own face in the glass, and was no more like myself than a statue is like the uncut stone. I was beautiful, and I was vain of the change. The gold embroidered gallant attire made me another man, and I marvelled at the magic of a few ells of cloth, fashioned to a certain device. The character of my clothes became my own, and in ten minutes I was sufficiently conceited.

Clarimonde watched me with a kind of maternal

fondness as I walked up and down the room, proving my new raiment, as it were; then,—

" Come," she cried, " enough of this child's play! Up and away, my Romuald! We have far to go; we shall never arrive."

She took my hand and led me forth. The gates opened at her touch; the dog did not waken as we passed.

At the gate we found the groom with three horses like those he had led before: Jennets of Spain, the children of the wind. Swift as the wind they sped; and the moon, that had risen to light us at our going, spun down the sky behind us like a wheel broken loose from the axle; we seemed to see her on our right, leaping from tree to tree as she strove to follow our course. Presently we came on a plain, where a carriage with four horses waited for us; and the postilion drove them to a mad gallop. My arm was round the waist of Clarimonde, her head lay on my shoulder, her breast touched my arm. Never had I known such delight. All that I had been was forgotten, like the months before birth, so great was the power of the devil over my heart.

From that date mine became a double life; within me were two men that knew each other not—the priest who dreamed that by night he was a noble, the noble who dreamed that by night he was a priest. I could not divide dreams from waking, nor tell where truth ended and illusion began. Two spirals, blended but touching not, might be a parable of my confused existence. Yet, strange as it was, I believe I never was insane. The experience of either life dwells distinct and separate in my memory. Only there was this inexplicable fact—the feeling of one personality existed in both these two different men. Of this I have never found an explanation, whether I was for the moment the *curé* of the village of ——, or whether I was *il signor Romualdo*, the avowed lover of Clarimonde.

Certain it is that I was, or believed myself to be, in Venice,—in a great palace on the Grand Canal, full of frescoes, statues, and rich in two Titians of his best period, we dwelt,—a palace fit for a king. We had each our gondola, our liveried men, our music, our poet, for Clarimonde loved life in the great style, and in her nature was a touch of Cleopatra. Custom could not stale her infinite variety; to love her was to love a score of mistresses, and you were faithless to her with herself, so strangely she could wear the beauty of any woman that caught your fancy. She returned my love a hundred-fold. She scorned the gifts of young patricians and of the elders of the Council of Ten. She refused the hand of a Foscari. Gold enough she had, she desired only love; a young fresh love herself had wakened,—a love that found in her its first mistress and its last.

As for me, in the midst of a life of the wildest pleasure, I should have been happy but for the nightly horror of the dream wherein I was a *curé*, fasting and mortifying myself in penance for the sins of the day. Custom made my life with her familiar, and it was rarely that I remembered (and that never with fear) the words of the Abbé Sérapion.

For some time Clarimonde had not been herself, her health failing, her complexion growing paler day by day. The physicians were of no avail, and she grew cold and dead as on the wondrous night in the nameless castle. Sadly she smiled on my distress, with the fatal smile of those who know their death is near. One morning I sat on her bed, breakfasting at a small table hard by; as it chanced in cutting a fruit I gashed my finger deeply; the blood came in purple streams, and spurted up on Clarimonde. Her eyes brightened, her face took on a savage joy and greed such as I had never seen. She leaped from the bed like a cat, seized my wounded hand, and sucked the blood with unspeakable pleasure, slowly, gently, like a connoisseur tasting some rare wine.

In her half-closed eyes the round pupil grew long in shape. Again and again she stopped to kiss my hand, and then pressed her lips once more on the wound, to squeeze out the red drops.

When she saw that the blood was staunched, she rose; her eyes brilliant and humid, her face as rosy as a dawn of May, her hand warm and moist; in short, more lovely than of old, and in perfect health.

"I shall not die! I shall not die!" she exclaimed, wild with delight, as she embraced me. "I shall yet love thee long; for my life is in thine, and all that is in me comes from thee. Some drops of thy rich and noble blood, more precious than all the elixirs in the world, have given me back my life."

This event, and the strange doubts it inspired, haunted me long. When the night and sleep brought me back to my priest's home, I beheld Sérapion, more anxious than ever, more careful and troubled. He gazed on me steadfastly, and said,—

"Not content with losing thy soul, thou art also desirous of ruining thy body. Unhappy young man, in what a net hast thou fallen!"

The tone of his voice struck cold on me; but a thousand new cares made me forget his words. Yet, one night, I saw in a mirror that Clarimonde was pouring a powder into the spiced wine-cup she mingled after supper. I took the cup, pretending to drink, but really casting the potion away beneath a table. Then I went to bed, intent on watching, and seeing what should come to pass. Nor did I wait long. Clarimonde entered, cast off her night attire, and lay down by my side. When she was assured that I slept, she uncovered my arm, drew a golden pin from her hair, and then fell a-murmuring thus,—

"One drop, one little crimson drop, one ruby on the tip of my needle! Since thou lovest me yet, I must not die. Sleep, my god, my child, my all; I shall not harm thee; of thy life I will but take what is needful for mine. Alas! poor love; alas! fair purple blood that I must drink! Ah, fair arm, so round, so white, never will I dare to prick that pretty violet vein."

So speaking, she wept, and the tears fell hot on my arm. At length she came to a resolve, pricked me with the needle, and sucked the blood that flowed. But a few drops did she taste, for fear of exhausting me, then she anointed the tiny wound, and fastened a little bandage about my arm.

I could no longer doubt it, Sérapion had spoken sooth. Yet must I needs love Clarimonde, and would willingly have given her all the blood in my veins that then were rich enough. Nor was I afraid, the woman in her was more than surety for the vampire. I could have pricked my own arm and said, " Drink; let my love become part of thy being with my blood." I never spoke a word of the narcotic that she had poured out for me, never a word of the. needle; we lived together in perfect union of hearts.

It was my scruples as a priest that disquieted me. How could I touch the host with hands polluted in such debauches, real or dreamed of? At night I struggled against sleep, holding mine eyelids open, standing erect against walls; but mine eyes were filled with the sand of sleep, and the wave carried me even where it would, down to the siren shores.

Sérapion reproached me often: one day he came and said,—

"To drive away the devil that possesses thee there is but one art; great ills demand harsh remedies. I know where Clarimonde is buried; we must unearth her, and the sight of the worms and the dust of death will make thee thyself again."

So weary was I of my double life, so eager to know whether the priest or the noble was the true man, which the dream, that I accepted his plan, being determined to slay one or the other of the beings that dwelt within me; ay, or to slay them both, for such a life as mine could not endure.

The Abbé Sérapion took a lantern, a pick, a crowbar, and at midnight we set out for the grave-yard. After throwing the light of the lantern on several tombs, we reached a stone half-hidden by tall weeds, and covered with ivy, moss, and lichen. Thereon we read these words graven:—

ICI GÎT CLARIMONDE,

QUI FUT DE SON VIVANT

LA PLUS BELLE DU MONDE.

*   *   *   *   *

"'Tis here!" said Sérapion, who, laying down his lantern, thrust the crowbar in a cleft of the stone, and began to raise it. Slowly it gave place, and he set to work with the pickaxe. For me, I watched him, dark and silent as the night, while his face, when he raised it, ran with sweat, and his labouring breath came like the death-rattle in his throat. Methought the deed was a sacrilege, and I would fain have seen the lightning leap from the cloud, and strike Sérapion to ashes.

The owls of the grave-yard, attracted by the light, flocked and flapped about the lantern with their wings; their hooting sounded woefully, the foxes barked their answer far away; a thousand evil sounds broke from the stillness.

At length the pick of Sérapion smote the coffin lid; the four planks answered sullenly, as the void of nothingness replies to the touch. Sérapion raised the coffin lid, and there I saw Clarimonde, pale as marble, her hands joined, the long white shroud flowing unbroken to her feet.

On her pale mouth shone one rosy drop, and Sérapion, breaking forth in fury, cried,—

"Ah, there thou liest, devil, harlot, vampire, thou that drainest the blood of men!"

With this he sprinkled holy water over my lady, whose fair body straightway crumbled into earth, a dreadful mingling of dust and the ashes of bones half burned.

"There lies thy Leman, Sir Romuald," he said; "go now and dally at the Lido with thy beauty."

I bowed my head; within me all was ruin. Back to my poor priest's house I went; and Romuald, the lover of Clarimonde, said farewell to the priest, with whom so long and so strangely he had companioned.

But, next night, I saw Clarimonde!

"Wretched man that thou art," she cried, as of old under the church-porch, "what hast thou done? Why hast thou hearkened to that foolish priest? Wert thou not happy, or what ill had I done thee that thou must violate my tomb, and lay bare the wretchedness of the grave? Henceforth is the link between our souls and bodies broken. Farewell! Thou shalt desire me."

Then she fled away into air, like a smoke, and I saw her no more.

Alas! it was truth she spoke; more than once have I sorrowed for her,—nay, I long for her still. Dearly purchased hath my salvation been, and the love of God hath not been too much to replace the love of her.

Behold, brother, all the story of my youth.

Let not thine eyes look ever upon a woman; walk always with glance downcast; for, be ye chaste and be ye cold as ye may, one minute may damn you to all eternity.

HOW WE TOOK THE REDOUBT.

(PROSPER MÉRIMÉE.)

A FRIEND of mine, an officer who died of fever in Greece, some years ago, told me this tale of his first battle. The story struck me so much that, as soon as I had the leisure, I wrote it down from memory.

"I joined my regiment at sunset, on September 4th. The colonel received me roughly enough, but his manner altered after he had read a letter I brought from General B——, and with a few good-humoured words he introduced me to my captain. The captain had just returned from a reconnaissance. I had scant time, as it chanced, to make this officer's acquaintance: he was tall, dark, and hard-featured, had risen from the ranks, and had won his commission and the Cross of Honour on the field of battle. There was a curious contrast between his almost gigantic height and the thin hoarse voice that he had spoken in ever since he got a ball through the body at Jena.

The captain smiled when he heard that I was just come from the military school at Fontainebleau.

"My lieutenant fell yesterday," said he, and I perfectly understood him to mean, "*You* will never fill his place." A tart reply was on my lips, but I kept it to myself.

About two gunshots from our bivouac, behind the redoubt of Cheverino, the moon was rising, large and red, as she usually is when she rises. But, that night, she seemed to me far bigger than common. For a moment the redoubt stood forth, black against the moon's disc, like the cone of a volcano in eruption.

"She's very red," said an old soldier hard by me;

"that's a sign the famous redoubt will cost some lives to take."

I have always been superstitious, and I felt the omen keenly. I lay down, but could not sleep; then I got up again and walked about for some time, watching the long lines of fire which covered the heights beyond the town of Cheverino.

When I thought that the fresh night air had cooled my blood, I came back to the fire, wrapped myself carefully in my cloak, shut my eyes, and never thought to open them again before daybreak. But sleep would not come near me. My thoughts grew black enough. I remembered that among all the hundred thousand men who covered the plain I had not a single friend. If I were wounded, I should be taken to a field hospital, and treated carelessly by ignorant surgeons. Everything that I ever heard about surgical operations rushed into my memory. My heart beat loud, and almost automatically I arranged my handkerchief and my pocket-book as a kind of breast-plate. Then fatigue overcame me ; every moment I dozed off, and every moment some ugly thought made me waken with a start.

At last my weariness had its way, and I was sound asleep when they beat to arms. We fell into our ranks, the roll was called, then arms were piled, and everything promised a quiet day.

About three o'clock an aide-de-camp rode up with an order; we took our arms again, our skirmishers scattered over the plain, we followed slowly, and at the end of twenty minutes we saw the Russian outposts fall back and enter the redoubt.

A battery of artillery took up position on our left, another on our right, both well in advance of us. They began a lively fire on the enemy, who replied with vigour, and the redoubt of Cheverino disappeared in clouds of smoke.

Our regiment was almost protected from the Russian fire by a shallow valley. They did not often aim at us, but rather at our artillery, and their balls passed over our heads, or at most knocked up gravel and earth into our faces.

As soon as the order to march had been given, my captain favoured me with a stare, which made me stroke my budding moustache once or twice with as careless an air as might be. I was not afraid, except perhaps of being thought to be afraid. The harmless cannonade helped me to keep up this heroic attitude. My vanity whispered that I was in real danger, being at last under the fire of a battery. I was delighted at feeling so cool, and thought how I would charm Madame de B——'s drawing-room, in the Rue de Provence, with the story of how we took the redoubt.

The colonel passed in front of our company, and spoke a word to me.

"You'll see something worth seeing for your first battle," he said.

I answered with a martial smile, and brushed

off my sleeve some dust from a ball which had fallen thirty paces off.

The Russians appeared to see that their artillery was a failure, for they now sent in some shells, which dropped more easily into the hollow where we were posted. A splinter knocked off my cap, and killed a man beside me.

"I congratulate you," said the captain, as I picked up my shako; "you're safe for the day."

I knew the military superstitions that *non bis in idem* applies in battle as well as in the law courts, and stuck on my shako with an air!

"It's an unmannerly way of welcoming folk," said I, as gaily as I might, and the joke seemed good enough in the circumstances.

"I congratulate you," said the captain once more. "You won't be touched again, and you'll get your company to-night. *My* goose is cooked. Every time I have been wounded, the officer next me has been grazed like you with a spent ball, and," he added with rather a shamefaced look, "their names always began with a P."

I passed it off with a jest; many people would have done the same, and probably many would have been as much struck as I was by the prophecy. A raw recruit, I felt that I must keep myself to myself, and must always appear perfectly cool and dauntless.

At the end of half an hour the Russian fire began to slacken, and then we sallied from our shelter to march on the redoubt.

Our regiment was composed of three battalions. The second was to watch the redoubt on the side of the gorge, the other two were to charge it. I was in the third battalion.

On leaving the ground that had covered us, we were greeted by some volleys of musketry which did a good deal of damage. The screams of the bullets took me aback. I kept turning my head, and my comrades, accustomed to the sound, laughed at me gaily.

"After all," I thought, "a battle is nothing so very dreadful."

We pressed on at the double, sharp-shooters in advance; suddenly the Russians gave three distinct cheers, and then waited, silent and holding their fire.

"I don't like their silence," said my captain; "it means no good."

I thought our own men were a little too noisy, and could not but contrast their clamour with the imposing silence of the enemy.

We reached the foot of the redoubt, where our fire had broken the palisades, and cut up the ground. Our fellows dashed over the ruins to the cry of "*Vive l'Empereur!*" You would not have expected men who had shouted so long to have shouted so loud.

I chanced to look up, and I shall never forget the sight I saw.

Most of the smoke had lifted, and hung like a canopy about twenty feet above the redoubt. Across a thin blue vapour you saw, behind their half-ruined parapet, the Russian Grenadiers, their muskets shouldered, motionless as statues. I think I see them yet; each soldier with his left eye on us, his right hidden by his musket. In an embrasure, some feet from us, a man with a lighted match stood beside a gun.

I shuddered, thinking my last hour had come.

"The dance is beginning," cried my captain. "Good-night!"

It was his last good-night.

The drums beat in the redoubt. All the muskets came to the level. I shut my eyes, and heard a terrible roar and crash, followed by cries and groans. Then I opened my eyes, amazed to find myself alive. The redoubt was blind with smoke. Dead and wounded men lay all around me. My captain was stretched at my feet, his head blown to pieces by a ball. I was covered with his brains and blood. Of all my company, there stood but six men beside myself.

After this carnage came a moment of stupor. The colonel put his cap on the point of his sword, and was the first man over the parapet, shouting "*Vive l'Empereur!*" All the survivors followed him. I scarcely remember what happened next. We got into the redoubt, I don't know how. Hand to hand we fought in a blinding smoke. I believe I kept striking, for my sword was all bloody.

"Victory!" I heard at last. The smoke thinned away; I saw dead men and blood all over the redoubt. The guns especially were littered with corpses. About two hundred soldiers, in the French uniform, were clustered anyhow, here and there, some loading their pieces, some wiping their bayonets. With them were eleven Russian prisoners.

The colonel was lying in his blood beside a

broken ammunition box. Some soldiers gathered round him eagerly. I joined them.

"Where is the senior captain?" he asked a sergeant.

The sergeant merely shrugged his shoulders.

"The senior lieutenant, then?"

"This gentleman who joined yesterday," said the sergeant stoically.

The colonel smiled a bitter smile.

"Come, sir," said he; "take the command. Fortify the gorge of the redoubt with those wagons, for the enemy is in force; but General C—— will support you."

"Colonel," said I, "you are badly wounded?"

"Done for, my boy; but we have the redoubt."

THE TAPER.

(LÉON TOLSTOI.)

" Ye have heard that it hath been said, An eye for an eye, and a tooth for a tooth. But I say unto you, That ye resist not evil."—*St. Matthew.*

IT was the time when the lords owned serfs. There were lords of different kinds. Some of them did not forget that there is a God, and that they would have to die one day. There were others who were dogs: may God have mercy upon them. But there were no worse masters than the old serfs, who had risen from the gutter and become masters in their turn. It was they more than any who made life hard to the poor people.

On a certain estate there was a land-steward. The peasants did the tasks which were set them. The lands were good and extensive, streams of running water, fields, forests. There would have been enough for every one—for the estate and for the Moujiks; but the lord of the manor had insisted on choosing a land-steward from among the servants of one of his other estates. The land-steward immediately assumed all authority, and weighed with all his weight on the back of the Moujiks.

He had a family, his wife and two daughters whom he had married, and he had already saved a great deal of money. He might have lived well and lived without sin, but he was insatiable, and already hardened in evil. He began by setting tasks which were unreasonably hard for the Moujiks. He built a tile factory, worked the people, men and women, up to the collar, and sold the tiles for his own profit. The Moujiks went to Moscow to complain to the lord of the manor; but it was of no avail. He sent them back, and allowed the steward to go on as he liked. The latter heard that the Moujiks had complained, and chose to revenge himself. Life became still harder for the peasants. Among them were some false brethren: they denounced their comrades, and strove to do harm to each other. But the people were stirred up, and the master's rage increased.

And as time passed, matters went from bad to worse, until the steward was hated and shunned like a wild beast. When he passed through the village, they shrank from him as from a wolf; they hid themselves anywhere to fly from the sight of him. The steward perceived this, and the fear he inspired increased his irritation. He began to overwhelm his people with blows and hard labour. And the Moujiks suffered.

It sometimes happens that such monsters are suppressed; the Moujiks began to talk of causing the disappearance of the master. They often met in a quiet nook, and the boldest would say: "Shall we bear any longer with our oppressor? A death for a death; to kill such a being is no sin."

One day there was a meeting in the woods, before the Holy Week : the steward had sent the Moujiks to prune the forest. They met at meal-time and held counsel. "How shall we live now?" they said. "He will uproot us root and branch. We are harassed. No more rest either day or night for us, or for our women. And the lash if he is not satisfied. Simeon died under the lash; Anissim perished in the stocks. What are we waiting for? He will come again this evening and have it out with us to his heart's content. We need but to drag him off his horse to give him a blow with an axe, and all would be over. We could bury him like a dog, and the water would run over his grave. Only let us be of one mind, let us all be steadfast! No backsliding!" So spake Wassili Minaev. He was more furious than any one against the steward. Wassili was beaten every week, and his wife had been taken from him to become cook to the steward. The Moujiks held counsel until his arrival.

He appeared on horseback, and picked a quarrel with the workmen because they did not prune trees according to his system. He discovered among the piles of cut branches a small linden tree. "I have not ordered the linden trees to be cut," said he. "Who has done this? Confess, or I will beat everybody."

He began to search for the row in which the linden-tree had stood. Sidow was pointed out to him. The steward slashed his face until it bled. He did the same to Wassili, under the pretext that his faggot was not big enough: and he left.

In the evening the peasants met once more, and Wassili spoke :—

"Well now, fellows, you are not men, but sparrows. 'We are going to settle his business for him!' you cried; and when the moment came, you backed out. It is in this wise that the sparrows unite against the hawk! No cowardice, no defection! And when he arrives, nobody budges. And then the sparrow-hawk comes, seizes what he wants, and away with it. Who is missing? Ivan. All the worse for him; serves him right; it is just like you. When one does not choose to draw back, he does not draw back. When he seized Sidow, we ought to have closed round him and finished with him. But you! No cowardice, no backsliding! And when he came, every one of you bent his head!"

Disputes cropped up more and more, and the Moujiks swore to rid themselves of the steward. He prescribed toil during the Easter feasts. This order irritated the peasants extremely. They met at Wassili's, in Passion Week, and began to deliberate again.

"If he has forgotten God," they said, "and acts in this wise, he must be killed, once for all. We shall die all the same if we do not do it."

Peter Mikhew came too. This Peter Mikhew was a timid man, and he did not like to be drawn into discussions. Still he came, listened, and said,—

"It is a great sin, my brothers, which you are premeditating. To lose one's soul is a grave matter. One can bear the loss of another's soul, but how about one's own? He does evil? The evil rests with him. It must be borne, my brothers."

Wassili waxed wroth when he heard these words.

"He is always repeating the same tale, 'tis a crime to kill a man! To be sure it is, but what a man! It's a crime to kill a good man, but such a dog! God wills it. Mad dogs have to be killed in mercy to men. It would be a greater crime not to kill him. How many men will he harm unless we do! And if we have to pay for his death, we shall suffer for others; they will bless us for it. You are talking nonsense, Mikhew. Will it be a less crime to work during Christ's feast? How about yourself— you would not go to work?"

And Mikhew answered,—

"And why not? If I am sent to it, I shall work. It is not for myself that I shall work, and God will know whose is the crime. It is not I who speak to put this, my brothers. Had it been said that we should resist evil by evil, God would have proclaimed it, but the contrary is said: If you strive to abolish evil yourselves, you take it on yourselves. It is easy to kill a man, but the blood will stain your soul. To kill a man is to steep one's soul in blood. You think to abolish evil by bringing a bad man to his death, but in truth you are burdening your own conscience with a worse evil. Bear with misfortune and you will conquer it."

After that the Moujiks came to no decision. Opinions were divided. Some thought like Wassili, others ranged themselves on Peter's side, to avoid sin, to endure.

The first day, Sunday, the peasants were allowed to keep the feast. The *staroste* * came in the evening and said,—

---

* A sort of representative of the peasants, chosen by themselves.

"Mikhail Simenovitch, the steward, orders that every one go to his work to-morrow."

The *staroste* went all through the village and announced the morrow's work to every one, assigning to some the lands lying on the further side of the river, to others those which bordered the high-road. They wept, the Moujiks, but they dared not disobey. On the morrow they took out their ploughs and began their labour. The church bells rang for mass; the whole world kept the feast; the Moujiks worked.

Mikhail Simenovitch, the steward, arose rather late, and took a turn on his land. His wife and his widowed daughter dressed themselves, a man-servant harnessed a little carriage, and they drove to mass. They returned; a servant prepared a samovar. Mikhail Simenovitch returned also, and they sat down to tea. After tea, Mikhail Simenovitch lighted his pipe and sent for the *staroste*.

"Well, hast thou set the Moujiks to their work?"

"Installed, Mikhail Simenovitch."

" Every one there ? "

" Every one is there. I conducted them thither myself."

" Installed, installed . . . are they working ? Go and see, and tell them I shall be there after dinner. They must drive a *déciatine* with two ploughs, and it must be well done. If I find any bad work, I shall not overlook it because of the feast."

" I understand."

The *staroste* was going to retire, but Mikhail Simenovitch called him back. He recalled him, Mikhail Simenovitch, he wanted to say something more, but he was embarrassed, he did not know how to begin: "This is what I mean. Listen, attentively, to what these brigands say about me. Who are they who menace, what they say, tell me everything. ·I know them, the rascals, they won't work. They would like to lie down doing nothing all day. Eating and drinking, that is what they like, and they do not consider that if we let seed-time go by it will be too late for anything. So listen to their chatter, and tell me whatever they may say. I must know all. Go, and hide nothing from me."

The *staroste* turned to go, went out and mounted his horse, and went towards the fields to the Moujiks.

The wife of the steward, having heard the conversation between the *staroste* and her husband, approached the latter, and asked him to grant her a favour. She was a gentle woman with a good heart.

Whenever she could, she calmed her husband's temper and defended the peasants against him. So she came to her husband and asked him for a boon.

"My friend Mickenka, for the great day, for the feast of our Lord, commit no sin, and for Christ's sake, do not make the Moujiks work."

Mikhail took no heed of his wife's words, and laughed in her face. "It must be a very long time since thy shoulders have felt the spanker, for thou hast become so bold? It is no business of thine."

"Mickenka, my friend, I have had a dream about thee, a bad dream; listen to me, don't let the Moujiks work."

"I tell thee thou must be too fat, and dost fancy the spanker won't slash thy shoulders. Take care! Take care!"

He got angry, did Simenovitch. He put the fire of his pipe close to his wife's mouth, sent her away, and ordered her to have dinner served up.

Mikhail Simenovitch partook of stew, pie, pork, *chtchi*,* roast sucking pig, milk soup with pasties in it, drank cherry-brandy, and finished up with a sweet cake. Then he called for the cook, and he ordered her to sing while he accompanied her on the guitar. So Mikhail Simenovitch passed his time gaily, striking the strings and jesting with the cook. The *staroste* entered, bowed, and proceeded to make his report.

---

* A sort of soup made of cabbage and beetroot.

"Well, they are working? Will they finish their tasks?"

"They have already done half."

"Is it well driven?"

"I have seen nothing wrong. They are afraid."

"Does the soil open up well?"

"Yes, very well; it crumbles like poppy-seed."

The steward held his peace for some moments.

"And what do they say about me? Do they call me bad names?"

The *staroste* appeared embarrassed. But Mikhail Simenovitch ordered him to tell the whole truth.

"Speak without fear. Thou wilt not pronounce thine own words, but theirs. If thou tellest the truth, I will recompense thee; but if thou hidest aught from me, I will beat thee. No offence meant. Ho, Katucha! give him a glass of brandy to encourage him."

The cook went to fetch the brandy, and handed it to the *staroste*. The *staroste* drank a health, swallowed the contents of the glass, wiped his beard. ("It's all the same to me," he thought, "it's all the same to me if they do speak ill of him; I will tell the truth, if he wants it.") And he began: "There is grumbling, Mikhail Simenovitch, much grumbling."

"But what do they say? Speak."

"They say that *he* does not believe in God."

The steward began to laugh. "Who said so?"

"Everybody. They say too that *he* is in league with the devil."

The steward laughed still louder.

"Good! But give me the details. Who says these things? What does Wassili say?"

The *staroste* did not like to speak against his comrades, but he had been on bad terms with Wassili for some time.

"Wassili cries out louder than any one."

"But what does he say? Will you speak?"

"I am afraid to repeat it. He says that *he* will not escape from the death of the damned."

"Oh, bravo! Then why does he wait instead of killing me at once? Are his arms too short? 'Tis well, Wassili; thou shalt have what is due to thee. And Tchika, that dog, he too, I suppose?"

"Every one speaks ill."

"But what do they say?"

"It is not well to repeat it."

"Where is the harm? Take courage. Speak."

"But they say: may his belly burst so that all his entrails may fall out."

Then Mikhail Simenovitch brimmed over with gaiety. "We shall soon see the entrails that will burst out first. Who said that? Tchika?"

"But nobody says any good; they all speak ill and threaten."

"Well, and Peter Mikhew, what does he say? He curses me too, I hope?"

"No, Mikhail Simenovitch, Peter does not curse."

"Then what does he do?"

"He is the only one of them all who says nothing.

He is strange. I looked at him with much surprise, Mikhail Simenovitch."

"And why?"

"All the Moujiks are astonished at his conduct."

"But what does he do?"

"It is quite an extraordinary thing. When I got near to him he was working on a sloping *déciatine* near Tourkine. I arrived where he was, and behold, I heard him sing in so sweet a voice, so pleasant . . . and on the plough something was burning."

"Well?"

"It burned like a little fire. I came up close to it, and I saw a taper of five *kopecks* stuck on the plough. The taper burned, and the wind did not blow it out. And he, in his new shirt, worked and sang psalms. He tilted the plough before me and changed furrows, and the taper did not go out."

"And what did he say?"

"Nothing. Only when he saw me, he wished me a good Easter, and began to sing again."

"Didst thou chat with him?"

"No. But the Moujiks came up then, and they laughed."

"Well," they said, "Mikhew can never pray enough to obtain pardon for the work done in the Holy Week."

"And what did he answer?"

"Only one thing: 'Peace on earth and goodwill unto men.' He turned back to his plough, pushed his horse on, and took to singing again. And the taper does not go out, but burns all the time."

The steward laughed no longer. He put down his guitar, let his head sink on his chest, and became absorbed in thought. He remained so for a certain time, then sent away the cook and the *staroste*, passed behind the screen, threw himself on his bed, and began to sigh and moan so loudly that it sounded as if a cartload of trusses of straw were passing. His wife drew near and tried to console him. He did not answer her. He only said: "He has conquered. But it has touched me."

"Go," she said; "leave them free. It will pass then perhaps. Thou hast done many such things, and thou hast never been so frightened. What dost thou fear now?"

"I am lost," he said; "he has conquered me. Go away, as I haven't yet killed thee; this is no business of thine." And he did not get up.

The next day he got up, and began to lead the life he had led before, but he was not the same Mikhail Simenovitch. He appeared to be oppressed by a presentiment. He pined away and hardly went out at all. He did not reign much longer. The lord arrived. He asked for him. The steward was ill. The next day he was still ill. The lord heard that he drank, and took the stewardship from him. Then Mikhail Simenovitch became quite inactive, became wearier and wearier, became dirty in his person and habits, and drank all his possessions, and fell so low, that at last he even stole his wife's kerchiefs for drink. Even the Moujiks had pity upon him and would give him drink. He died at the end of the year from drink.

THESE LOTS TO BE SOLD.

(EDMOND ABOUT.)

HENRI TOURNEUR, who had just won a first-class medal at the *Exposition Universelle*, was not a painter of genius, but his pictures were, without exception, excellent. He drew nearly as well as Ingres, and his colouring was nearly as rich as that of Diaz. His painting had been the rage for four or five years, and he had no need to fear the caprice of fashion. He sold at English, *i.e.* exorbitant, prices. The "*Visit of Court Ladies to the atelier of Jean Goujou*" was purchased for eighteen thousand francs for a Parisian museum. A banker of Rouen had given six thousand francs for the "*Kiss of Alain*

86

Chartier," kit-kat size, and "*Mdlle. Doze Listening to the Confessions of Mdlle. Mars*" was bought for eleven thousand francs by a wealthy Belgian amateur. He had (at the time at which this history opens) orders for more pictures than he could paint in two years, and there was nothing to prevent his making an income of fifty thousand francs.

His first success began with the exhibition of 1850. Till then he had earned his bread in obscurity. M. Tourneur, senior, a commission agent in wines, retired on £400 a year, had neither helped nor hindered his son's vocation. He had left him to himself without money, but with the following words of encouragement: "If you have any talent, you will help yourself; if you haven't any, you will give up painting, and I will start you in business."

From the age of twenty to thirty, Henri made woodcuts for cheap illustrated editions; he painted fans, bonbon-boxes, china, and even fire-screens. *L'enfant au pot-au-feu* was one of his youthful errors.

Those ten years of ill-paid work were of service to him. They taught him economy. When he could make sure of his daily bread for eighteen months, he turned his back on commerce and began to paint seriously.

He chose the largest studio in the *Avenue Frochot,* and one of the finest in Paris, and for a very simple reason turned it into a sort of museum, in which you would have found a little of everything except pictures. When Tourneur wanted to paint a Louis XII. lady sealing a love-letter, he began by visiting the curiosity shops: he would buy, either a piece of tapestry of the time, or a stamped leather hanging for the back-ground of the picture, and he would send home with it a fine specimen of con-temporary furniture. He would discover a richly incrusted little cabinet in a dark little shop, buy it, and carry it away under his arm. The costume would be painted from antique silks and from lace handed down through several centuries. He would bid at public sales for Marion Delorme's writing-desk, and for the seal of Ninon de Lenclos. Such was his love of accuracy. His dummy was dressed with scrupulous care, a fine model found for the face and hands, and everything painted from nature. At Tourneur's you would never light upon those slight or finished sketches or daubs, nor that fascinating confusion of half-finished studies, *impressions*, and unsold pictures one likes to meet with in a studio; but only one picture in process of painting and already framed, for he never painted but one picture at a time, finished it without interruption, and only kept it until it was varnished. But his walls were covered with splendid hangings, and bristled with costly arms. The antique furniture and *étagères* were crowded with porcelain, faïence, grès de Flandres, precious enamels, rare bronzes, and artistic goldsmith's work. His house was a miniature museum, like a branch of the *Musée de Cluny*.

As to his personal appearance, if you had not

seen his portrait engraved by Calamatta, he would not have attracted your attention had he passed you in the street. With his regular, rather cold features, his very fair complexion, light chestnut hair, and whiskers worn in the English fashion of the year 18—, you would rather have taken him for a young British merchant than a well-known artist.

Although he was of small stature, he was well proportioned and remarkably well dressed in the finest and best-cut cloth. He neither indulged in eccentricities of form or colour, nor in any jewellery but his Breguet watch. If he carried a stick, it would be a five-guinea cane, with a tortoise-shell knob worth a few pence. I have often met him in the days when he was his own valet, and I never remember seeing a speck of dust on him. He often went to bed without dinner, but he never went out with dirty gloves, and when he took his meals at a dairy in the Rue Pigalle, he had his boots and his hats in the Rue Richelieu. In his studio he wore white cotton in summer and woollen in winter, which was always spotless; he was as clean and neat as his painting. An Englishman, on his way home from Egypt, had left a young Nubian lad of eighteen behind him in Paris. The Englishman had even forgotten to give him a name. Tourneur allowed himself the luxury of taking him into his service and christened him *Boule-de-Neige*. He instructed him in those liberal arts that are within the compass of black races, such as polishing a *parquet*, dusting furniture, brushing clothes and boots, carrying letters to their destination, and was soon (thanks to this system of education) the best valeted man in Paris, for the sum of ten francs per month. It was then said of him that he had already saved a great deal of money; but I, who knew him well, can assure you that this was not the case. Artists have a way of exaggerating everything, and especially the savings of other artists. Tourneur had spent too much on purchases of every kind to be rich in coin of the realm. And take into account, if you please, that *Boule-de-Neige* devoured three *kilogrammes* of bread daily, which will help you to perceive why at this date his master's fortune amounted to no more than fifty thousand francs, or two thousand pounds invested in government stocks.

However modest this sum may appear, it must prove to every reasonable person that M. Henri Tourneur was a well-conducted artist. He frequented neither balls nor theatres, with the exception of the *Comédie Française*, where he had a free pass. At thirty-five his habits were as regular as those of a man of his age could possibly be. Still, I will not assert that he was indifferent to the beauty of Mellina Barni. When she broke off her engagement with the director of La Scala to come and sing in Paris, it was he who persuaded her to put off her *début*. You might often have met him at her house, and, what is more significant, you sometimes met her at his. But that is no business of mine.

On the 15th of May of the year 18—, an hour after the opening of the *Exposition des beaux-arts*, Henri Tourneur was absorbed in the contemplation of his own work and, smiling at his picture of *Alain Chartier*, when he experienced one of those friendly and familiar digs in the ribs that would disturb the equilibrium of a bull. He turned round as if a spring in him had been touched, but his anger could not withstand the broad smile on M. de Chingru's red face; he burst out laughing.

"Bonjour, Van Ostade, Micris, Terburg, Gerard Dow!" cried M. de Chingru, in so loud a tone that five or six people had the advantage of hearing his remarks. "I have seen *thy* three pictures, they don't lose any of their charm, they are magnificent; in fact, there is nothing else here. You have beaten France, Belgium, and England; Meissonnier, Willems and Mulready. You paint *genre* as well as Genro himself, and you are as learned as *Pinxit*. If the government doesn't order a hundred thousand franc picture of you and give you the Cross of the Legion of Honour, I shall pull the *Bastille* about its ears!"

He caught hold of Henri's arm, and added in a whisper,—

"Would you care to marry?"

"Leave me alone, will you?"

"A million?"*

"You are mad, a million wouldn't have me."

"Why not? A million and you are of equal value. What is the yearly interest of a million? fifty thousand francs. You can make as much as that. You are therefore worth a million."

"But where did you discover that?"

"Ah, ah! the tale interests you. Well, listen. Once upon a time there was, there still exists, a certain Monsieur Gaillard. . . ."

"Who gambles on the Stock Exchange. No, thank you. I have seen the play of *Ceinture dorée.*"

---

* Forty thousand pounds.

"He no more gambles than I do; he is a clerk at the * * * office . . ."

"With a salary of ten thousand francs."

"With a salary of three thousand six hundred, besides a never-failing gratuity of four hundred francs, total four thousand. There is your future father-in-law."

"And my million ?"

"Ah, *my* million ! You nibble, Van Ostade, you nibble ! Monsieur Gaillard is a model *employé*. For the last thirty years he has arrived at his office at five minutes to ten, and left it at five minutes past four, and he doesn't leave his hat to represent himself in the interim, whilst he goes to play at billiards."

"Chingru, you are intolerable."

"Patience ! To resume, this model clerk, this phœnix of *employés*, lives in the Rue d'Amsterdam, with his daughter, his sister, and his *bonne*. Their apartment is on the fourth floor, three bedrooms, no sitting-room. The windows . . ."

" Good-bye, Chingru."

" Ta-ta, Gerard Dow. Their window overlooks ten thousand square *mètres* of land. You are still there ? "

" Go on ! "

" Ten thousand *mètres* at a hundred francs, make a million. Whoever denied this fact would be at direct variance with Pythagoras ! This million, my dear Terburg, is the property of M. Gaillard."

" But how did he get it ? "

" Don't be alarmed; he hasn't stolen it. A purse may be stolen any day, but an acre or so of land cannot be stolen; there are no pockets big enough. In the year of grace 1830, a few days after the events of July, M. Gaillard, a supernumerary of five years' service, found himself in possession of seventy-five thousand francs, the inheritance of an uncle in Narbonne. He was looking out for an investment that no revolution could touch, when he discovered those lucky plots of land, then worth seven francs per *mètre*. He soon made his calculation, seventy thousand francs for the purchase of land, five thousand for lawyers' fees, and taxes. He paid money down, and thereby gained some further advantage."

"But since, why hasn't he sold?"

"Since? He has never even taken down the board, and I will show it you whenever you choose. *'This site to be sold, as a whole or in lots.'* And please to observe that purchasers have not been wanting. The day after the signature of the deed he was offered a profit of ten thousand francs. He said to himself, 'Humph! I haven't made a bad bargain,' and he kept his land. When the railway station was built at Saint-Germain, a speculator offered him two hundred thousand francs. He scratched his nose (it is his only bad habit) and replied that his wife did not wish to sell. In 1842, his wife was dead : a gas company made him the most dazzling overtures; half a million ! ' *Ma foi*,' he replied. ' As I have waited twelve years, I may as well go on waiting. I am too well satisfied with the way time works for me to interfere. When my daughter is marriageable, we shall see what we shall see !' I may as well tell you that his daughter is a contemporary of his landed property. In 1850, his daughter was twenty, a charming age, and his land was worth eight hundred thousand francs, a good price. But he is so accustomed to keep both of them that it would take a crusade to decide him for either marriage or sale. It is useless to insinuate that the two cases are not parallel, and that whilst building lots are none the worse for waiting, girls after a certain age are apt to become less marketable; he stops his ears and returns to his desk, where he continues his conscientious scribble."

"And his daughter ? "

" She bores herself at the rate of a hundred francs

per day, with all her heart, in fact to such an extent that she will fall in love with the first man who appears above the horizon."

" She never sees any one ? "

" No one who can be described as a human being. An old country lawyer and five or six government clerks, with grave and clerkly manners. You see a man doesn't give balls in an apartment consisting of three bedrooms. I am the only presentable man who has access to the house."

" She isn't too ugly ? "

" She is magnificently beautiful ! that is all ! "

" Has she a human name ? I warn you that if she is called Euphrosyne——"

" Rosalie; what do you say to that ? "

" Yes, Rosalie—Rosalie—a pretty name. Has she any sort of education ? "

" She ? An artist, my dear fellow, to her fingers' ends, like you and me."

" Like which of us ? be good enough to specify."

"Monster of ingratitude! She doesn't play any musical instrument, and she doesn't copy the pictures in the Louvre; but she understands painting, and appreciates music as if she had invented it. Oh! a most severe education; four concerts during Lent, the play six times a year, public buildings twice a month, a subscription to a serious library, few novels and all English, no doves in the house, not a cousin in the family!"

"Go on, Chingru, I can bear with you! And when will you introduce me?"

"To-morrow, if you like. I have already spoken of you to her."

"And what have you said about me?"

"That among all our great painters you were the only one of whom I possessed no picture."

"I will begin you one to-morrow."

"Thanks; and now I am going to ask you for another service——"

"If it's not a service of plate——"

"You know, my dear fellow, that I am nearly forty, and have no occupation. At my age a man ought to be settled, most men are. I don't like to be an exception to the rule, and to hear people whispering about me: 'Monsieur de Chingru, a good name. What does he do?' 'Oh, nothing; he has private means—a man who never asks you for anything.' 'Yes; but what does he do with himself and his time?' *Parbleu!* I would do just like everybody else, if I only had a post of say three thousand francs! Look here, my dear fellow, I don't ask you for anything now; but later, if you are satisfied. You have a certain influence—you know influential people, you visit at Cabinet Ministers' houses. You'll say a good word for me, won't you?"

"What can you do?"

"Anything, for I haven't confined myself to any special study."

"Well, I won't say no. What time to-morrow?"

"At two o'clock. She will be alone with her aunt. You will call about the purchase of a ' site.' "

" Shall I call for you ? "

" No, no; I will call at your studio. I am never at home. Do you even know where I live ? "

" I don't quite remember."

" There, I told you so ! Well, all my friends are in the same proud position. I don't live any-where, I perch. I am so little at home, that I hardly know my own address ! Ta-ta."

Monsieur de Chingru (Louis Théramène), of no occupation, and of no known habitat, was what is commonly called a studio-pest. He had a talent for ingratiating himself with artists by swinging a gigantic incense burner under their noses, and by pooh-poohing the one to the other. He would establish himself in their studios on terms of *tutoiement*, and would manage to pick up and carry off such crumbs as a sketch or a study. Without being either an artist or a critic, he had the instinct of a picture-dealer, and had a certain faculty for singling out au unsuccessful picture. In the studios where he had the *entrée*, he would pose himself against the wall like an exclamation stop, extolling everything good and bad alike, until he pitched upon the picture for which the artist cared the least. He would then bring all the weight of his admiration to bear on it; he would make for it with all the impetuosity of his enthusiasm; he would leave it, but to return to it; he would compare a master-piece to the object of his dominant passion 'to the disadvantage of the former, then he would take his leave. But he would fix his last regard on the object of his desire.

The next day he would again appear, but this time without noticing any one; he would hardly pass the time of day; but would go straight to the same picture. That would be his pole, and he would be drawn to it as by a magnet. He would not hesitate to say to the artist: " Behold *thy* first masterpiece. The day you achieved this you achieved greatness. Before, you were merely a painter of the calibre of Delacroix, Troyon, or Corot; after this you became yourself, *tu étais toi*."

· And he would look at it again, and take down the frameless picture, carry it to the window, dust it tenderly with the back of his sleeve, and put it back in its place, with many a sneer against the Philistines who refrained from covering it with gold. He would return a week later, but to look in another direction; that corner would be avoided, or his eyes would only wander as if there against their owner's will, while he stifled a sigh.

One morning he would arrive with the sun. He had dreamt that his beloved picture was sold to the Queen of England. He wanted to gaze on it once more. Then the artist had but to lose patience, and break into invective :

"*Thou* art but an ass ! Here are twenty not too contemptible pictures, and you go into an ecstasy over a daub. That sketch is idiotic. Nothing can ever be made of it. I don't ever want to see it again. Take it away, but don't ever mention it again to me."

Chingru never waited for this to be said twice to him; he would rush to the picture with inarticulate cries of delight, and hold it up for the artist's contemplation; then pæans of praise to the painter, and a signature would be obtained that trebled its value. No one much minded giving him a picture, because it was known that he possessed a good many by good masters; it was not derogatory to add to his collection. But where was his collection? Nobody had ever seen it. His dwelling was like the lion's cave; you might know what went in, but never what came out of it. All the pictures bestowed on him were immediately sold to a dealer, who sent them to the provinces, to Belgium, or to England. If chance brought back one to Paris, then Chingru unblushingly declared that he had given it away.

"I am too good-natured and easy-going to keep anything for myself;" or else, "I exchanged it for a Van Dyck."

What painter would complain at having been exchanged for a Van Dyck? Thus did Louis Théramène de Chingru create for himself a Benevolent Association among the studios of Paris. Henri Tourneur had never given him anything for the best of all reasons. If you can sell your paintings, why should you give them away? But he promised himself he would repay him generously if he served him well in this affair of the marriage.

On the morrow both were punctual, and the clock of the railway station of the Rue St. Lazare was just striking two when Chingru pulled Monsieur Gaillard's bell. The old aunt had gone to market with the *bonne*, and it was Rosalie who opened the door. She led them into the dining-room, answered Chingru's inquiries about her family, allowed Monsieur Tourneur to be presented to her, received him as a man of whom she had heard a great deal, and listened graciously to what he had to say about the choice of a site, and the construction of a studio. She did not know under what conditions her father intended selling, nor whether he would consent to divide a single plot; but she showed a lithographed plan, which Henri asked permission to take away with him for a day or two: he would call again to arrange with Monsieur Gaillard. The interview lasted ten minutes, and the painter went away dazzled.

"Well?" questioned Chingru on the staircase.

"Don't talk to me; my eyes smart. It seems to me as if I had been in Italy."

"You are not very far out; the dynasty of the Gaillards has its root in Narbonne, a Roman city. *Père* Gaillard boasts a descent from the conquerors of the world. You would humiliate him severely by attempting to prove to him that his name is but a very French adjective, which has attained the dignity of a surname; and if, following the tradition of comic opera, you were to accost him with, '*Bonjour, bonjour, Monsieur Gaillard!*' he would start an endless dissertation to prove to you that there once existed soldiers, or camp-followers whose duty it was to take charge of the helmets, *galea*, helmet, *galearius*, hence Gaillard; Vegetius on Tactics, chapter and verse so and so. That is how you are listening to me."

Henri's eyes were fixed on the house of Monsieur Gaillard. Chingru continued,—

"Don't give yourself all that trouble; her windows look out the other way. So you approve of her?"

"She is not a woman, Chingru; she is a goddess. I expected to see a poor Eugénie Grandet, worn by privations, and dried up by melancholy. I could not have believed her to be so tall, so well grown, of such splendid beauty, and with such dazzling colouring. You said she was five-and-twenty. Yes, she must be five-and, twenty, the age of perfect womanhood. All the Greek statues are twenty-five!"

"Brrr! whirr! You are off like a covey of partridges. Did you notice her eyes?"

"I saw everything—her large, dark eyes; her beautiful chestnut hair; her divinely drawn eye-brows; her proud mouth, with the full, red lips; her little transparent teeth; her pretty taper hands; her strong, rounded arms; her foot, no bigger that my hand, and no wider than my two fingers; her ear as pink as a shell. Did I see her eyes! But I even saw her dress, which is of English alpaca; her collar and sleeves, worked after her own design; for you would not find that sort of pattern in a shop. She wears no rings on her fingers, and her ears are not pierced. *Thou* seest, I know her by heart."

"*Diantre!* If the heart has already begun to

speak, there is nothing more for me to busy myself about."

"I must have talked a lot of nonsense. I did not hear what I said; I lived in my eyes; I revelled in the contemplation of perfect beauty for the first time in my life."

"That will do. Now come and contemplate something else."

"What?"

"The land for sale."

"What do I care for the land! If that girl is penniless, and she will have me, I will marry her!"

"Do no violence to your feelings, my dear fellow; if the property is in your way, you can hand it over to me. I have often regretted that I was not born a landed proprietor."

When M. Gaillard returned from his office, Rosalie informed him that M. de Chingru had brought a young artist, M. Henri Tourneur, to see the land; that she had given him the plan; that the latter gentleman would call again to see him.

"But," she added, laughing, "I suspect he is thinking of something else, for he only looked at me; he didn't know what he was talking about. And, besides, he is much too good-looking for a mere would-be purchaser."

Monsieur Gaillard did not frown; he only scratched his nose (a handsome nose), and made answer,—

"Monsieur de Chingru should mind his own business. I shall call to-morrow morning to get my plan from that young man, and find out what he wants of us."

II.

At eight o'clock next morning, Henri was in the act of slipping on his painting coat, when Boule-de-Neige introduced a very tall, very thin, very polite, and rather timid man, preceded by a magnificent nose. It was Monsieur Gaillard. He sat down, and proceeded to explain with much circumlocution that his land had been divided once for all, for the greater convenience of purchasers; that it would be impossible to divide a lot equally, because each lot had only fifteen *mètres* of frontage; that there would be great difficulty in calculating the value of the remaining fraction, which would not look out on the street; and if Monsieur Tourneur was disinclined, or unable to buy a whole lot, part of which he could dispose of later, why it would be better to let the matter drop.

"Sir," replied Henri, almost as intimidated as his

interlocutor, "I am neither a very sagacious purchaser, nor a very experienced vendor. I am an artist, as you see, M. de Chingru, . . . but, really! I don't see why I shouldn't speak plainly to you, although what I have to say is not easy to explain. Sir, you are not only a landowner; you are a parent. What I had heard of your daughter inspired me with an unconquerable desire to know and speak to her. That land was my pretext. I must confess that I chose a moment in which I hoped to find her alone. I took her by surprise, and had the honour of a ten minutes' conversation with her. She is as marvellously beautiful as she is charming and well-bred; and as you have just accorded me an interview, I should have solicited to-day or to-morrow, permit me to inform you that my highest ambition is to obtain the hand of Mademoiselle Rosalie Gaillard."

M. Gaillard's hand hurriedly found its way to his nose. Henri continued:

"I am aware how unusual is such a point-blank and sudden proposal. You can hardly know my name. I am thirty-four years old; the public like my painting, and pay me well for it. I have invested a sum of fifty thousand francs in five years, and besides have saved enough to purchase the furniture you see here, which is worth about the same sum. I can prove to you that I have eighty thousand francs' worth of orders, which I shall complete before the first of January, 1857, without any undue haste. This to my credit, as my father would say. As to the debit side of my account, I do not owe a farthing. I might put down my father's fortune to the good, ten thousand francs per annum, honourably gained in commerce; but although I mention it, I do not choose to count on it. My father has the admirable habit of leaving me to my own resources. I shall not ask him for a marriage portion. On the other hand, if you honour me by granting me your daughter's hand, I should entreat you to keep all your fortune for your own use; I will undertake to support my wife and children. I do not attempt to blind myself to the fact that these conditions are far from equalizing our relative positions. To this end I should have to be richer or you poorer; but I know no means of enriching myself in a day, and I am not egotistical enough to desire your ruin. I think I can guarantee that by the time your daughter comes into possession of her property, I shall be so well off that I need not blush for the addition an unearned million—— I don't know, sir, if you understand me."

"Yes, sir," replied Monsieur Gaillard; "and although you are an artist, you appear to me to be an honest man."

Henri Tourneur blushed up to the eyes.

"Pardon me," said the worthy man, with some feeling, "I don't want to talk badly of artists; I don't know them. I only wanted to express to you that you argue like a straightforward man, like a clerk, a merchant, or a lawyer, and you don't profess the slipshod morality of other members of your profession. Besides, your appearance is in your favour, and I think you would please my daughter if she saw you often. She always had a decided taste for painting, music, embroidery, and all such little accomplishments. Your age is suitable to Rosalie's. Your disposition seems to me satisfactory, being at the same time serious and cheerful. You seem to be a good man of business, and I should think you were capable of administering a considerable fortune. In a word, sir, you please me, and for this reason I have to request you not to come to my house, sir, until you hear from me again."

Henri felt as if he were falling from the spire of Strasburg. After pausing to take breath, Monsieur Gaillard hastened to take up the thread of his discourse:

"I wouldn't say this to you if I looked upon

you as a nobody, like Monsieur de Chingru. But I am prudent, sir, and in your interest, as well as in my daughter's, I must make inquiries about you. I believe that your conduct is all that could be desired; but if you happened to have any connection that later on might disturb my daughter's happiness, you are not likely to enlighten me on the subject, are you? You tell me you make a mint of money, and I believe it, although it seems to me extraordinary for one man to be able to manufacture eighty thousand francs' worth of pictures in eighteen months. I believe you, but for the satisfaction of my conscience, I must make inquiries. I must have a talk with your respected father, to ascertain if he has ever had cause to complain of you. It would be well for me to inform myself in the neighbourhood if you have any debts——"

"Sir——"

"I believe all you have said, but sometimes one

has debts without knowing it. Where were you educated?"

"At the *Collège Charlemagne, Institution Jauf-fret.*"

"Good! I shall call on the heads of the *Collège* and at the house of the professor where you boarded. I will do nothing underhanded, but I am a cautious man, sir. It is my strong point, or my weakness, as you choose. I have no reason to complain of it. Had I been less cautious, I should have sold my property to the Saint Germain Company in '36. That would have been a pretty business! Had I been a frivolous parent, like many others I could name, I should have bestowed my child last year on a stockbroker, who blew his brains out the other day. Patience, young man; you will lose nothing by waiting. If you are worthy of my daughter, she shall be yours; but business is business. I am prudent. You needn't come to the door with me. If my father had been as prudent as myself,

I should be a richer man than I am. Go back to your work: go on with it. I am a cautious man!"

Henri spent a week in executing variations on the well-known theme: Hang caution and all cautious men! But he acted with prudence and promptitude in breaking off his acquaintance with Mellina. He sent her a grand piano which he had promised her, and told *Boule-de-neige* that henceforward he was not at home to her.

Chingru came on the eighth day to announce M. Gaillard's visit to him. He informed him that M. Gaillard had been all over Paris, had interviewed all the government officials (especially those of the *Beaux-arts*), questioned all the picture dealers, ransacked the catalogues of previous exhibitions, re-read the five last *Salons* of Théophile Gautier, and collected a vast amount of information. "He knows everything; he knows that you got a fourth-class history prize at the general competition on the organization of Roman Colonies; he is greatly touched by this fact. He came to me on a more personal and delicate matter: I need not say that Mellina's name was not mentioned."

Monsieur Gaillard arrived at half-past four. He began the conversation by a hearty shake of the hand, that rejoiced the painter's heart. "My young friend," said he, "I have been to see forty or fifty different people, who have told me a great deal about you: it now remains for me to study you a little myself. I should have no objection to your becoming better acquainted with my daughter; for if you marry any one, it will not be me, after all. We ought to see each other every day for two or three months. After that time we could talk of business."

Henri thanked him enthusiastically. "How good you are, sir! you authorize me to pay my court to Mademoiselle Rosalie?"

"Oh dear no, not at all! Don't be too hasty! Why, the very idea would scandalize my household! A young man as a visitor every evening! And if the affair fell through, all Paris would know that Monsieur Henri Tourneur had paid his addresses to Mademoiselle Rosalie Gaillard, had contemplated marriage with her, and that the engagement had been broken off. People would want to know why; they would invent reasons; who can foresee what gossip it would give rise to?"

Henri managed to restrain a movement of violent impatience. "Sir," said he, "do you know of any other place where we could meet each other every day?"

"Faith, no; and that is what puzzles me. Think it out. You are young, you say you are in love: it is for you to find a means!"

"If it were a question of half a dozen interviews, there would be the theatres or concerts; but one cannot go to such places every day

An idea!   I may not go to you, suppose you come to me ?"

"Young man! with my daughter ?"

"Why not? I am an artist, and therefore a privileged person. Have you never seen any studios ?"

"No; this is the first——"

" Allow me to call your attention to the fact that an artist's studio is neutral ground, a place of public resort, shady in summer and heated in winter. You enter it at any hour; you leave it when you are tired of it; you make appointments there, and you meet your friends. The master of the house receives visitors from early morning till sunset. Strangers passing through Paris visit the studios as they do the palaces and churches, without tickets of admission, with the sole obligation of bowing when they enter, and expressing their thanks when they leave. And then it is generally the artist who expresses the thanks."

"But I don't choose all France and hordes of foreigners to march past my daughter!"

"Is that your only objection? I will shut my door to every one but you."

"But even then our visits must have a plausible pretext."

"Nothing simpler: I will paint her portrait."

"Never, sir! I am incapable of accepting——"

"You shall pay me for it!"

"I am not rich enough to permit myself such a freak."

"Perhaps you think a portrait is an expensive object?"

"I know the price your pictures fetch."

"Pictures, yes, not portraits. I hope you don't take a portrait for a picture!"

"What difference is there?"

"Oh, a great difference, my dear Monsieur Gaillard. What makes the value of a picture; is it the paint? No! Is it the canvas? No!

It is its composition. Pictures are dear only because so few men can compose them. But in a portrait invention is useless, nay worse than useless, dangerous; you have but to copy your model faithfully. Any painter can produce a portrait. A photographer, a common workman who may neither read nor write can produce an admirable portrait in ten minutes, price twenty francs, frame included. In the face of this competition, we have been obliged to lower our prices; the pictures make up for the loss in portraits. If you take a turn on the *boulevards,* you will see the price of portraits marked up everywhere. They are no longer sold, they are given away, fifty francs for a small one; a large one costs a hundred francs, but the frame is not included!"

"That would not be an obstacle, but what would my friends say if they saw my daughter's portrait by the celebrated Henri Tourneur in my possession?"

"You would tell them you had had it painted on the *boulevard.*"

"You promise not to sign it?"

"I promise anything you please. When shall we have the first sitting?"

"Listen to my plan: I have a right to a fortnight's holiday every year with full pay. I have not availed myself of this right for two years; I was saving up the time for a tour in Italy. So, by arranging with my chief, I can take a holiday of six weeks. Give me five or six days to arrange the matter decorously. I don't care to startle a whole department: I am a prudent man."

He then went away, leaving the painter to the happy contemplation of the vanity of human wisdom. "Here" (said he to himself) "is a worthy paterfamilias, bringing his daughter into the lion's den of a painter's studio from prudence."

It is not possible to define the hold a fine studio may take upon a woman's imagination;

that is to say, a painter's studio, for the cold,
the damp, the pails of wet plaster, the harsh
tones and the all-permeating dust of the marble
spoil the charm of even the finest sculptor's studios.
If a painter has taste and is well off, you are
dazzled the instant you set foot on his threshold.
An abundant light straight from the sky
plays with its stuffs, its tapestries, the cos-
tumes hanging on its walls, the antique furniture
and trophies. A person accustomed to ordinary
furniture, where everything has its legitimate use,
is delightfully bewildered by this ordered disorder. His glance wanders from one object,
from one mystery to another; probes the depth
of the great oaken cabinets; glides lightly over
the polished surfaces of Japanese or Chinese
ware; rests here on a quiver full of long arrows,
or a large two-handed sword; there on a
Roman cuirass covered with the rust of twenty
centuries. A stringless guzla, a hunting horn

enamelled with verdigris, a pifferaro's flute, a rudely painted tambourine, become objects of interest and curiosity. For an intelligent woman (I think all women are so) all these trifles must have a meaning, every piece of tapestry tells its own tale, every old beer pot has its *lied*, every Etruscan vase its romance, every steel blade its epic. All those arrows must have been dipped in *curare*, that South American poison which would kill with a prick of a pin. Those lay figures crouching in corners are so many sphinxes, who are silent only because they would have so much to say. The possessor of all these marvels, the king of this luminous empire, cannot be a man like ordinary men. When he is seen, smilingly hospitable in the midst of all those hieroglyphs which he can decipher, he compels admiration. Whatever be his garments they add to the charm. They are sure to please as an original mode of dress, free from the follies of fashion, and in perfect keeping with his surroundings. If he is clothed in cotton, the Indies must have furnished it; if in flannel, it has been woven in Scotland from Australian wool: you would never dream of its coming from the *Belle Jardinière*. A pair of red slippers bought in the Rue Montmartre transform themselves into *babouches* from Cairo or Beyrout. The little sleeping room, through whose open door you may catch a glimpse of an Algerian bedcover, almost suggests a harem. One would be only half surprised if five or six odalisques, bearing amphoræ and water-bottles, were to step out of it. Even the faint smell of the varnishes and other essences has its share in the hallucination. Add to this a few drops of Malaga in a Venetian glass, and Rosalie Gaillard, who had never drunk anything but water in her life, might imagine herself to be many thousand miles away from Paris.

The first sitting was a decisive one. Henri had transplanted the whole stock of a Neuilly florist into his garden; banks of flowers bloomed even in the studio. "If I visited at her house," he thought, "I should always take her a bouquet; she shall not be the loser because I cannot do so." Rosalie, like all *Parisiennes*, adored flowers and had lived for many years on the hope of having a garden of her own. By a singular caprice of nature this child of uncultured parents had every instinct of refined luxury. She would rather have done without bread than music, and she believed flowers to be more necessary than boots or shoes. Her eyes shone at the sight of a fine equipage, although the only carriage she had driven in was an omnibus. She loved dress without ever having indulged in it; every night she danced in her dreams, although she had never been to a ball; she bought all the parks and country-houses that she saw advertised on the fourth page of the *Constitutionnel*. With these tastes, she would have been much to be pitied had she not been buoyed up by certain well-founded hopes. The privations of her existence, and the crushing of all her instincts, might have embittered her to the heart's core, and given to her mind the grey tint of old maidism. But she was conscious of her father's fortune, and being sure of the future, found her consolation in looking out at that great piece of bare land which formed her mental horizon. She had taken as her motto: *Un temps viendra !*—a day will come—and she lived on hope. She had built herself a delicious retreat in her innermost soul. Nothing was wanting there, not even the love of a handsome young man, who was sure to present himself. Thus sustained, she bore patiently the household drudgery, the making of her own clothes, the conversation of her father's friends, and the eternal game of piquet with which they enlivened their evenings. During the last year M. de Chingru had appeared upon the scene as an intermediary, to be classed between those worthies and people of "society," just as in the animal world the monkey is placed between the dog and man. As soon as she saw Henri Tourneur, she decided that he was her fate; she had no need to seek further. His person, his garden, his talk, and his studio represented absolute perfection to her; and had any one said to her, " There are better fish in the sea," she would have thought he was laughing at her.

The painter, while sketching a full length portrait of Rosalie, studied in every detail the perfect beauty which had dazzled him at first sight. He did not find his judgment at fault; for you must be something of an artist to guage the beauty of a young girl. The glamour of youth, the freshness of tint, and a moderate *embonpoint* often compose a sort of unreal and temporary beauty that disappears in the matron. One may have married an adorable young girl, and yet be tied for life to a plain woman. Real beauty does not lie in the epidermis, but in the structure, whence it may be deduced that a really beautiful woman is beautiful for life, despite the external ravages of time. Rosalie had the unalterable beauty that need fear no wrinkles and can defy all time. Those who have travelled in Italy can easily picture her to themselves when I say that she was like a Roman girl with small feet.

The ice was soon broken, to the great astonishment of Monsieur Gaillard, who no longer recognised his daughter. He had never seen her so full of life; she had never been so bright or such a chatterer. Rosalie yielded herself up without constraint to the influence of this love, whose course ran so smoothly. She ran from studio to garden and from garden to studio; she looked at everything and touched it; she questioned, laughed, and chirped like a thrush at the vintage. Her youth, so long kept under, burst forth; she was again fourteen. Henri, rather more reserved, lived in a kind of ecstasy. After having passed through the privations to which poverty and economy had condemned him, here was heaven raining every delight, wealth, and happiness at once upon him. During the past fifteen years he had made several pleasant but expensive acquaintances, and he could not believe in the good fortune which granted him the love of a girl at once prettier and wittier than any he had known. He had foreseen the possibility of marrying for money, as a soldier in the midst of a campaign might foresee the *Invalides;* but he had never invested the fortune in his mind's eye with so much beauty, neither had he ever heard of a million with such small hands and such large eyes. Joy lent its light to his by no means remarkable face, and he was positively handsome for about two months. Rosalie beheld in him an inspired artist when, in the intervals of a sitting, he took his violin and played the prettiest and gayest airs from the *Noces de Jeannette* or the *Trovatelles.* Monsieur Gaillard played his part of nuisance conscientiously. He insisted on being talked to by Henri Tourneur. The good man belonged to that deplorable tribe of ignoramuses who insist on learning at an age when it is too late to learn. Infatuated with Roman history as a schoolboy becomes infatuated with entomology or conchology, he had read and re-read two or three volumes of superannuated erudition; he quoted them on every occasion, interrogating, discussing, seeking, in fact, as he phrased it, to extend the modest field of his acquirements. Henri paid him the attention due to the age, fortune, and position of a future father-in-law. When he was tired of dissertation, and the young people would return to the chapter of their love and their hopes, he would soon take up the thread of his discourse again and embark on endless admonitions that might all be concentrated into, "Don't fall too much in love; you know that nothing has been settled."

Notwithstanding these minor precautions, Henri's

studio was a little earthly paradise with *Boule-de-Neige* for its guardian. Monsieur de Chingru attempted to force its entrance several times; he divined a sort of mystery. But *Boule-de-Neige* always informed him with brazen imperturbability, "Massa gone out," "My massa dine out," or "Good little white man gone country, hunt animile, draw gun, *boum*." His master had taught him a language somewhat resembling the picturesque tongue of the immortal Friday. Instead of sending him to school where he would have learnt French, he took upon himself the task of instructing him. Sometimes he would say to him, "Take care not to become too learned, nor to talk like other people; you would go off in style and colour!" And *Boule-de-Neige* was anxious to keep his colour, to his mind the finest colour in the world.

The portrait was finished by the time Monsieur Gaillard's holiday ended, towards the end of July. Of course it was not allowed to go to the framer's, where a score of artists might have seen it. A workman came to measure it, and three weeks afterwards brought home a twenty guinea frame, for which M. Gaillard paid one louis, without bargaining. As he happened to be there, he also disbursed the fifty francs for the portrait, for which he took a receipt.

The following Sunday, he invited all his friends to a beer and hot patty soirée: they comprised an old notary from Villers-le-Bel, three old commission agents, Rosalie's writing-master, and an ex-manufacturer of masks and foils who had retired from business on a yearly income of three thousand francs. The invitation was for half-past seven. At nine, Monsieur Gaillard announced a surprise: he carefully withdrew the shade from the lamp, while his sister, drawing aside a green curtain, disclosed the portrait of Rosalie. There was an unanimous cry of admiration:

"What a splendid frame!" cried the ex-manufacturer.

"Oh, but it's the portrait of your young lady!" said the notary.

"And how like!" said the chorus of government clerks.

"That's my way of doing things," said Monsieur Gaillard, as he imprinted a kiss on his daughter's brow.

"If I may take the liberty of making a remark," began the writing-master, who had been silent as yet, "why did not Monsieur Gaillard wait till the fourth of September, the day of St. Rosalie, so that Mademoiselle might have had this surprise for her *fête?*"

"Because I am preparing another for her birth-day," answered Monsieur Gaillard firmly.

"To be sure, you can afford it," said the chorus.

"Might one venture to ask," said the notary "what sum this image cost you?"

"Seventy francs, frame included."

"It is expensive, but not dear. And whom is it by?"

"It's by no one particular; it's a mere portrait."

"That," said a deep voice which caused every-one to start, "is a Tourneur, second manner, and is worth 8,000 francs."

Monsieur Gaillard sank into his chair as if he had been struck by a thunderbolt.

"Good evening, Papa Gaillard! Ladies, I have the honour! Gentlemen, I am your very devoted!" added Monsieur de Chingru, whom the *bonne* had admitted without waiting to announce him. "It is deucedly hot."

"The weather is heavy," said the panting notary.

"There is electricity in the atmosphere," re-marked the writing-master, breathing heavily.

"It will rain to-morrow," said the chorus.

The conversation continued on this theme until ten o'clock. Monsieur de Chingru retired, followed by all the others. There had been a regular scandal at Monsieur Gaillard's.

Next morning, Chingru presented himself at the studio and was admitted by *Boule-de-Neige* : he related the adventure of the previous evening, and warmly congratulated his friend. "After such a sensation," said he, "the affair is safe enough. The ancient Roman has passed the Rubicon. Accept my heartfelt congratulations. If it hadn't been for me——"

"I know what I owe you, and I shall not forget it."

"Faith, my dear fellow, if you mean to be grateful, here's a fine opportunity. I have also discovered a golden alliance for myself."

"*Peste !* there seems to be enough for every one !"

"A splendid business, I tell you. . . . I have begun to pay my court."

"Bravo !"

"But there are preliminary expenses, the deuce and all, bouquets, presents, and just now I haven't a penny."

"I thought you had a good income."

"I can't get my rents in. Ah, my dear friend, may Heaven ever protect you from farming tenants!"

"Do you want money? Here."

"Two hundred francs! what do you think I can do with two hundred francs?"

"Well, you can buy a good many bouquets with them; but if you need five hundred, call again at twelve o'clock and I will give you the rest."

"My dear good fellow, I am grieved to find that we have not nearly hit upon the right figure. If you wanted to be useful to me, you would have to lend me ten thousand-franc notes."

"For your bouquets?"

"For bouquets and other things. Can't you

trust me? Am I not good for ten thousand francs?"

"Softly! don't excite yourself. You know that I look forward to marrying at any moment. I have declared my fifty thousand francs; if they are not forthcoming, Papa Gaillard would make a row."

"You could give him my security."

"Oh, that alters matters! If you give me security, I have no objection to make. Where is your property?"

"A mortgage! Who do you take me for? One gives a mortgage to an usurer; but I thought a signature would suffice between friends. I offer *thee* my signature!"

"Thanks!"

"You refuse?"

"Positively."

"You don't know what might happen to you."

"*Advienne que pourra*—Come what may!"

"Your marriage is not yet an accomplished fact."

"What do you mean? And what do you dare to insinuate?"

"I will give you twenty-four hours for reflection. If to-morrow . . ."

The painter heard no more. He opened the door, seized Chingru by the shoulders and hurled him horizontally on to a bed of hortensias, that never raised their heads again.

III.

Monsieur Gaillard burst into lamentations after the departure of his friends. His daughter and sister consoled him as best they could. "What does it matter?" said old Mademoiselle Gaillard. "Sooner or later we should have had to announce the marriage to them."

"What marriage?"

"Mine, papa," said Rosalie boldly.

"You talk as if it were settled. Thou art afraid of nothing, rash child!"

"One would indeed be a coward to be afraid of happiness."

"You really love this young artist?" The word *artist* could not shape itself easily between those venerable lips.

"I believe that I love him with all my heart."

"It is not enough to believe, one should be sure. There is yet time for reflection; to weigh the pros and cons."

"They have been sufficiently weighed, my father."

"Do you not feel the necessity of collecting your thoughts for a month or two before so serious a crisis?"

"I have been collecting my thoughts for the last twenty-five years and three months, my dear father."

"Oh, these children! If this marriage is to take place, you will commence by signing me a holograph declaration; that is to say, one written entirely in your own hand, that it is your desire to marry Monsieur Tourneur."

"I will sign with two hands, dearest father."

"In this way, I free myself from all responsibility, so that if, ten years hence, you were to come to me and say: 'Why have you married me to an artist?' I should be able, with the proof in my hand, to say: 'It was your own wish.'"

"I shall never complain to my best of fathers. But what have these poor artists done to you that you judge them so severely?"

"There is no denying that they form a caste outside society. I understand manufacturers, who produce, merchants who distribute produce, soldiers who make their nation illustrious, and functionaries who administer it. The artist's orbit is outside all that. The Romans, our ancestors, held him in no esteem; they looked upon him as an excrescence of the social body."

"Fie on those ugly set phrases! When poor Henri shuts himself up in his studio with his canvas and his panels, what does he do?"

"What does he do? Nothing worth talking about; he manufactures pictures."

"Ah! I have you there. He manufactures. He is a manufacturer. A painter is a manufacturer of pictures. He produces painted canvas, as your friend Monsieur Cottinet used to produce the visors of helmets!"

"That is quite another thing!"

"There I agree with you. And when he has finished a picture, what does he do with it—does he warehouse it?"

"No; he sells it."

"Of course he sells it! He exhibits his merchandise, he distributes his produce, he gives an impetus to trade; he is a merchant."

"You are playing on words."

"By no means; I am arguing. And when he

has created a hundred masterpieces (for he *does* create masterpieces), what will the world say of him? The world will say, 'Paris has the honour of having given birth to the celebrated Henri Tourneur; Henri Tourneur, whose paintings have humbled the pride of old Holland, and made modern France illustrious.' That is well worth a sub-lieutenant's epaulette. The minister has promised him that he will be decorated in two years. Now, what do *you* mean by glory?"

"It is no good talking; it is not——"

"No, no, I will not spare you a single syllable; and you must hear me out. You talk of functionaries; but Henri is ten thousand times more of a functionary than you! Functionary, indeed!"

"Ah! I should like you to explain that to me."

"What is a functionary? A man in the service of the State, and who is paid out of the Budget. The more he is paid, the greater the functionary.

And now, since Henri has received an order for work to last him a year from the State, is he or is he not in the service of the State? And when, at the year's end, he goes to the treasury to receive forty thousand francs, isn't he ten times a bigger functionary than you, who only receive four thousand francs?"

"You great baby! this proves clearly——"

"That you must marry me to my dear Henri if you wish me to marry a manufacturer, a merchant, and a functionary all rolled in one!"

"But, you tyrant, have I even the time to think of your marriage? There is my property to think of again. Now they want to build a *cité-ouvrière* on it. I have seen the list of the members of the committee—all good people. They sent to sound me through one of my chiefs. I should get a million, money down, and they would leave me a plot of twenty *mètres* by fifteen to build upon. It is a very good offer. What shall I do?"

"Accept it, as it is such a good offer."

"But in ten years it would be superb!"

"But in a hundred years, papa, it would be magnificent! 'Tis true that neither you nor I would be any the better for it."

"All this is too much for me. Good-night; I am going to bed."

"Without coming to any decision, papa?"

"I shall sleep over it."

And the worthy man did sleep, as was his wont, a deep and sonorous sleep, the noise whereof sometimes imitated the rumbling of thunder, and sometimes the roll of a stage-coach across a bridge. He possessed two precious gifts, which the heaviest cares could never imperil—appetite and sleep. Next morning he sallied forth to his office, more irresolute than he had ever yet been, but sustained by a couple of pounds of bread and an enormous bowl of *café-au-lait*.

He had hardly reached the Rue Saint Lazare,

when his daughter and his sister heard the most formidable rat-tat which had ever burst upon the house in the memory of bells. Rosalie ran to the door, crying,—

"Something has happened to papa!"

The bell-ringer was Monsieur de Chingru, wearing a coat buttoned up to his chin, and a great air of important secretiveness. He was admitted by Rosalie and her aunt, who, like provincials, were dressed by eight o'clock every morning. At nine, the traces of breakfast had disappeared, and the dining-room was transformed into a working-room.

"Ladies," said Chingru, "pardon me for disturbing you at this early hour. It is in your interest that I call to acquit myself of an honest man's duty. It is I who brought Monsieur Henri Tourneur here, with regard to some land he was supposed to intend purchasing. May I yet be permitted to arrest the consequences of my imprudence while there is yet time?"

"Speak, sir; explain yourself at once," said Rosalie.

"Mademoiselle, you can bear me witness that I have always spoken of M. Henri Tourneur in flattering terms."

"You have; and what more have you to say?"

"I told you, your aunt, and your excellent father that Tourneur was an artist of talent, a good-natured fellow—in fact, what we men about town call a thoroughly good fellow. I looked upon him as a friend, and my opinion of him has not altered. If you were to question me about him on those points, I should still give you the same answer. But why did I not learn sooner that your respected father entertained other ideas— that he contemplated marrying you to him? Certainly, I shouldn't have cried out, 'Do not marry him; he is not worthy of you. You will be sorry for it some day.' No; I am not the sort of man to betray a friend. But I should have spoken to you gently, in your own interest. I should have said, 'There is this obstacle: some women would shrink from it, others might think nothing of it. It is for you to decide if you can battle with a certain person, and the memory of an intimacy of long-standing and mutual pledges, and—er—other consequences. If you can hope to be the winner, why, then, marry!'"

Monsieur de Chingru had no sooner spoken than he reaped the fruits of his discourse. The tears did not fall down Rosalie's cheeks; they burst forth as if impelled by an invisible force. But that was only for an instant. The brave girl stifled her grief.

"Thank you for your kind intention," she said, "but we knew all,"—adding, to mitigate the effect of her too transparent fiction,—"Monsieur Tourneur has confided the history of this connection to us; and besides, as you know, everything is broken off!"

"I should think so, Mademoiselle, as much as——"

"That is enough, sir; and if no further un·fulfilled duty detains you here——"

"I—if you—you understand, Mademoiselle, that, placed as I was, between the necessity of speaking or of holding my tongue——"

"You held your tongue when you should have spoken, and you spoke when you should have held your tongue. Good-morning, sir."

And thus was Monsieur de Chingru dismissed.

At four o'clock in the afternoon of the same day Monsieur Gaillard was putting his pens, his pen-knife, and his black cotton sleeves away in his desk, when a fine, tall woman, as yellow as an orange, invaded his office.

"Monsieur," she cried, with a very marked accent, "*he* is a monster! I loved him, I love him still. For him I have left my country, my family, and the *teatro della Scala*, where I was *prima donna*

assoluta. He is going to be married. He aban-
dons me and our two poor children, *Enrico* and
Enrichetta. What a monster, sir, an unnatural
father! I forbid you to give your daughter to
him! My dear Gaillard, thou hast the air of an
honest man; promise me that thou wilt not give
thy daughter to him! I am mad, *vois-tu.* Understand me well, my good Gaillard. I don't know
French, *mi spiego male;* but thou seest I have no
longer my head, that I am . . . If he marries
her, *l'ammazzero* . . . I will kill him and his
wife; I will kill myself afterwards; I will set fire
to the church, and I will go and do penance in
Rome! Swear to me that thou wilt not give thy
daughter to him."

Monsieur Gaillard bowed his head under a storm
of words, in which Italian and French formed an
agreeable mixture. He interpreted as best he could
this medley of exclamations, and learnt that his
future son-in-law had betrayed and abandoned

Mellina Barni. Having done his best to console the fair disconsolate, he wrote, on the spur of the moment, the following note, which he despatched by a *commissionnaire* :—

"Paris, *this Monday, 30th July,* 18—, *a quarter-past four.*

" Sir,—

"Mademoiselle Mellina Barni has honoured me by a visit at my office. I need say no more to you. This young lady appears to me to be a most interesting person, and I am not so inhuman as to wish to separate her from the father of her children.

"Deign to accept, sir, the assurances of my most distinguished consideration.

"Gaillard."

The signature had a most masterly flourish. The paper was that fine, smooth, thick, heavy, lined, and lordly paper which the Government provides expressly for the use of its offices and the correspondence of its officials.

Henri Tourneur did not take note of so many details. He hastily got into his clothes, took up his cane, and rushed off to Mellina, who received him with open arms.

Mellina was an ethereal-looking, tiny blonde, as white as a drop of milk. She spoke French without any foreign accent, as a proof of which she was preparing to make her *debut* in an exquisite little three-act piece of Meyerbeer's at the *Opéra Comique*.

She wore a white *peignoir*, and was rehearsing a magnificent *Allegro*. To her great surprise, Henri rated her soundly, and taxed her with having taken liberties with his name. She neither knew Mousieur de Chingru nor Monsieur Gaillard. She had divined that Henri had given her up because he intended to marry, and although she had a right to feel aggrieved, nothing would have induced her to put obstacles in the way. The intervention of the two children made her furious. She was indignant at having, through no fault of hers, been made to play the part of the *Limonsine* or *Picarde* in *Monsieur de Pourceaugnac.* She could hardly be restrained from accompanying Henri to Monsieur Gaillard's house, and the painter had some difficulty in persuading her that the cure would have been worse than the disease. He went straight to the Rue d'Amsterdam, and found the door shut against him. *They* were at the play, at least the servant said so. He went there every evening for a week, and always met with the same answer. He went by day. They were at a concert. So many plays and concerts were equivalent to a formal dismissal. If he had met Monsieur de Chingru on the stairs as he turned away, the chances are that he would have torn him to pieces. He wrote to Monsieur Gaillard, and then to his sister. All his letters were put in envelopes and returned to him. He lost patience, and rushed to the Courts, where he interviewed the Recorder on duty, a young man of thirty, precociously initiated in every mystery of Parisian life.

"Sir," replied the magistrate, "this is not the first case of the kind which has come before the law-courts. You must have heard of those matrimonial agencies, whose proceedings are sometimes tolerated and sometimes put down by our tribunals. There exists, besides the great houses who parade their prospectuses, a class of individuals whose sole profession is to run to earth large fortunes, colossal *dots*, and any kind of money-bag that inhabits a fourth floor, and take toll of them. They are leagued together, and form limited companies, whose only capital is intrigue, and whose statutes have never been published. Some of them exact ten per cent. on a marriage-portion; some are satisfied with a moderate commission, for there, as everywhere else, you meet with competition. M. de Chingru, whatever be his real name, has certainly proved one of the moderate of them. When he found himself baulked, he had the little scene you describe played by one of his partners, or rather accomplices. We will endeavour to trace the actress and the author of the piece, but it is unlikely that a woman of whom you have such a slight account will be discovered; and were she found, it would be difficult to prove the connivance of Chingru."

When the painter got home, he found the following missive, dated from Havre, awaiting him :—

"MY POOR TOURNEUR,—

"If I had offered to give you 990,000 francs and an adorable wife into the bargain, you would have ranked me with the gods. I was stupid enough to put the matter in a different form before you ; I offered you a million, of which ten thousand francs were for me. You lost your temper, and you suffer for it. I have wreaked an artistic vengeance. Monsieur Gaillard believes you to be the father of two children and the quasi-husband of a yellow woman! 'Tis a blow from which you will never recover, my poor Tourneur! But pray, when you threw me on to those hortensias, was I on a bed of roses ?

"Chingru & Co."

Henri was proceeding to tear the paper to shreds in a moment of rage, but as he was *blond*, he altered his mind : " Chingru, good Monsieur de Chingru," thought he, " you are going to make it up between Monsieur Gaillard and me! I need but oblige him to read this letter."

He coaxed Chingru's letter into a big envelope, sealed it with an enormous cornelian seal, whereon were graven the arms of Ninon de

Lenclos, and wrote the address in a bold, round hand:

"*A Monsieur*,

"*Monsieur Gaillard, Archiviste,*

"*Au Ministère de——*"

Monsieur Gaillard opened the letter as respectfully as if he were breaking the seal of a government despatch. Chingru's signature piqued his curiosity: he had resolved to return Tourneur's letters, but not Chingru's. This singular document completely reversed his ideas; he accused himself of cruelty and injustice, and asked for permission (for the first time in thirty years) to leave his office at two o'clock!

Rosalie bedewed Chingru's signature with her tears. "I knew it," she said; "and had you allowed me to influence you, you would have given poor Henri a chance of defending himself!"

Then they all, Rosalie, her father, and her aunt, agreed to go to him to his studio the following day by way of making amends. This was certainly due to him. Rosalie was wild with happiness.

"Why, I believe you loved him all the time?" questioned her father.

"More than ever. Something whispered to me that he had been calumniated."

Suddenly the door opened, and the servant announced Mademoiselle Mellina Barni. Rosalie and her aunt had barely time to escape into the next room. I don't know what they conversed about when there, but I believe that it would have been difficult to pass a hair between Rosalie's ear and the door leading to the dining-room.

Monsieur Gaillard contemplated the real Mellina like a child gazing at a magic lantern. For a moment he thought a conspiracy to mystify him had been hatched, and that a new Mellina Barni would be sent to him every day. He began to think of changing his residence, without leaving an address behind him.

Mellina had great difficulty in persuading him that her name was really Mellina Barni, that she was nineteen years of age, that she was not the mother of a family, that she lived with her mother, and that she had not come to complain of Monsieur Henri Tourneur. She explained to him in excellent French that her conduct was exemplary, and that she had left the theatre of *La Scala* to appear at the *Opéra Comique*. She informed him that ladies of the theatrical profession can pay visits, receive presents, and see their friends, without either compromising or being compromised. She owned that she had loved Monsieur Henri Tourneur, and had hoped to marry him; but that since the middle of last May, he had left off paying her visits, and had honourably put an end to a connection which had been honourable throughout.

"I will not say, sir," she added, "that I renounced my hopes without regret; but this is a fate to which we must all submit. We are all more or less courted by rich young gentlemen who admire us sufficiently to make love to us, but who do not love us well enough to marry us, and who, when they are sure of our virtue, turn their backs upon us— to wed elsewhere. This is precisely the history of Monsieur Tourneur; and because a tale has been told you which is neither to his credit nor mine, and you have shut your door to him, and because I know that he is ill from grief, I have summoned all my courage and come to you. I hope you will know how to distinguish between truth and falsehood."

When Mellina went away, Rosalie ran back to her father. Perhaps she would have preferred that Chingru's falsehoods had not been founded on fact, and yet I am not sure that Mellina's visit produced a bad impression on her. Mellina had appeared very pretty to her through the keyhole, and she forgave the painter for having been in love with her. She knew that a girl who married a man past thirty had always some rivals in the past, and she preferred not to have ugly ones; nineteen women out of twenty would be of her opinion. She felt, from the ring of Mellina's voice, that she spoke the truth, and that there had been nothing to blush for in this love. Besides, she could no longer doubt that she had dethroned the beautiful Italian about the middle of May, that is to say, at first sight.

But Monsieur Gaillard was once more overwhelmed with perplexities. He would certainly not call on Monsieur Tourneur; he reproached his daughter for the obstinacy of her affection.

"I am willing to own," quoth he, "that this young man is not so black as he has been painted; but he has associated with actresses. *Qui a bu boira!* I would as soon think of trusting a dipso-maniac. You believe he will be faithful to you, but he abandoned that young Italian; he might just as well play you the same trick. Besides, we must not think about this marriage until my land is sold."

When he was advised to sell his land, he answered,—

"There is no hurry; I shall sell it to give my daughter a marriage portion, and my daughter isn't married yet."

The sight of the portrait annoyed him; it vexed him to be under an obligation to Henri Tourneur.

"What shall we do with this accursed portrait?" he asked Rosalie. "We cannot keep it after a rupture. Suppose we send it back to him?"

"How can you think of such a thing, papa? I should be for ever in his studio."

"To sell it and send him the proceeds would be indelicate. Whom could I give it to? I do not choose either to give or sell my daughter's portrait. It might get into the hands of the trade, and at every sale at the *Hotel Dronot*, I should tremble to read in the paper : 'Portrait of Mademoiselle R. G., by M. Henri Tourneur, price 8,000 fr.' I would rather scrape the paint off with my own fingers."

"Destroy my portrait,—all that remains to me of the happiest moments of my life!"

"Hold thy peace. Dashed painter, dashed Chingru! dashed property! I would give it to any one who would take the trouble off my hands! Had we not been so rich, all this would never have happened!"

Monsieur Gaillard lost his appetite; he ate like an ordinary man. His sleep became much lighter and infinitely less noisy. He was no longer punctual at his office; twice he got there after ten. This was on the 17th and 18th of August. When he came home, Rosalie's old aunt remarked to her:

"Your father must have thought a great deal; his nose is quite red on one side."

Henri left off working; he lived on the pavement

of the Rue d'Amsterdam. Monsieur Gaillard carefully avoided him, and he did not dare to accost Monsieur Gaillard. He would have dared to speak to Rosalie, but she never went out without her father. At last, on the 3rd of September, he received a note from Monsieur Gaillard inviting him to call on him to receive the remaining 7,950 francs that were still owing for the portrait. He would be expected to be there to receive the money at five o'clock. He accepted this strange invitation, not for the sake of the money, but of Rosalie. The three principal founders of the *cité ouvrière* were met at Monsieur Gaillard's at the same hour to settle the business of the purchase of M. Gaillard's property. The worthy man had declined all responsibility in the matter; he left all to Rosalie, and she had treated with the purchasers. Henri arrived just as the notary was reading the last clause of the deed of sale.

" The purchasers agree to build on Lot F, belonging to the vendor, a dwelling house for Monsieur

Gaillard and his family, with a painter's studio on the first floor."

Monsieur Gaillard looked at his daughter, who looked at Henri, who looked at no one. He was terribly pale, and leant against the wall.

"*Allons,*" said the worthy man, taking up his pen, "here is a flourish that will put an end to all my cares!"

"Monsieur," remarked the notary, "yours is a remarkably fine handwriting."

A CONVERSION.

TH. BENTZON.

I.

"Here's a letter for *M. le Curé*,"* said a little fellow in wooden shoes, who stood at the open door of the presbytery.

The servant, busy, washing in her kitchen, wiped the snowy lather off her hands and took the paper held out to her.

"*M. le Curé* is reading his breviary; shall I disturb him? Is an answer required?"

"I don't know," said the boy; "I was told to wait."

---

* Parish priest.

She signed to him to enter and sit down, while with the lagging step of age, she bent her way towards the garden.

A *curé's* garden, in very deed, with its little narrow, box-bordered walks, wherein to walk and cherish abstract thought, and the high walls that separated it from everything external, except the highest cross of the neighbouring burying ground.

The black foliage of a yew tree marked the angle of the flower beds, which were varied with plots of vegetables, the whole carefully tended by *Monsieur le Curé* himself. For he did not disdain, by way of recreation, to turn up his cassock, and dig and delve. On the sunny, ivy-garlanded curb-stone of the old well a fat cat lay rolled up, mingling its purr of enjoyment with the faint hum of the bees which buzzed, as if intoxicated, above and around the flowering lilies, whose perfume loaded the air of a burning August afternoon. In an arbour, where a statue of the Virgin gleamed white in the shade, *Monsieur le Curé* had sheltered himself from the sunbeams which came down in a rain of fire from a cloudless sky.

With his head resting against the leafy hedge, the clear-cut sunburnt profile standing out like an antique from the dark background, he sat and meditated, with one finger between the leaves of his book. For the last five years, although he looked so young, this hour had found him regularly absorbed in the contemplation of the daily duties of his office, thinking of the good still to be done, ever dissatisfied with himself, although he lavished his time, his strength, and the little money he possessed, without stint. The circle wherein he spent his untiring activity was a very narrow one. Without even owning it to himself, his ardent spirit suffered from the curb. His vocation would have drawn him towards the life of a missionary or of an army chaplain, for there was something of the soldier in him, the taste for heroic adventure.

But the father of the Abbé Fulgence, a tiller of the
soil in his own vineyard, had given his only son
to God on condition of not losing sight of him
altogether, and of his incurring as little danger as
possible. The sublime aspirations of this parish
priest were checked for the time being by his filial
obedience. He had not renounced the dreams of
his youth as far as the future was concerned. He
harked back to them involuntarily, while he
laboured on without respite but without much
success, teaching and catechising the village
scamps. The grief nearest his heart lay in the per-
ception that he could only hope to succeed in
instilling the bare letter of religion. Not that
either men or women neglected attending mass;
but that their apparent devotion was merely due to
routine, and neither cured this one of avarice, nor
his neighbour of drunkenness, nor did it prevent their
marriages from being often merely an act of tardy
justice. To awaken the enthusiasm of virtue in

these gross natures would have been an impossible task. The inhabitants of Arc-sur-Loire vegetated from their cradle to their grave, greedy for gain, solely pre-occupied with the hoarding of their savings, quick to envy their neighbour's harvest, bent double with the toil of wringing its produce from the soil, without seeking aught beside; neither better nor worse, taking all in all, than other peasants, and superior to many of them in that they could read and write. The midland departments of France are supposed to be enlightened, but their lights, as they do not bear on spiritual matters, were far from satisfying his heart's desire. He had not yet made any of the conquests his ambition had promised him; the good and evil around him were devoid of grandeur, or rather could hardly be said to exist. All the sheep of his flock had the same uniform, unmeaning expression. There were neither harassed consciences nor fruitful repentances. There was no question of high aspirations; they all dragged their steps iu the common path without other pre-occupation than the constant struggle for daily bread. And yet far away there were the heathen to convert and sinneis to save!

A zeal as ardent as it was wasted possessed the Abbé Fulgence. He towered alone of his kind above his commonplace surroundings, as an oak raises itself high above the undergrowth that threatens to choke it. And, iudeed, the comparison to a noble oak suggested itself naturally in the presence of the physical and moral solidity of features, the voice, the whole person of a singularly striking individuality. There was none of the ordinary shy mannerism of an ecclesiastic at the outset of his career, fresh from the seminary.

The steel grey eye of the Abbé Fulgence bent on the women of his flock a regard whose frankness was marred by no timidity. If you had ventured to suggest to him that some of them remarked the fine presence of *Monsieur le Curé*, the brilliant smile which sometimes brightened the usually pensive expression of his regular features, or the thick-black, curly hair, where the tonsure made a small bluish circle, he would have betrayed by a curt or indifferent answer the secret contempt which a priest,—who has absolutely abjured all things mundane,—feels for the sex whose very weakness is treachery, for the eternal stumbling-block in the way of pious resolve; a contempt certainly veiled and softened by charity, but therefore deeper, because unmixed with fear. The temptations of the Abbé Fulgence came from a higher plane; they urged him forward to far-off apostolic perils. He would have chosen martyrdom a hundred times in preference to the tedious, inglorious drudgery imposed upon him by the present hour. His feelings might have been compared to those of a youthful bride, who, having built up a romance of her own, suddenly finds herself imprisoned within the icy walls of a marriage of convenience.

"*Monsieur le Curé!*" said the voice of Ursula, the old servant, standing two steps away from him.

He did not hear her.

The Abbé Fulgence was passing over in his own mind for the hundredth time that chapter of disappointments which each of us bears more or less legibly imprinted on our conscience, and which might be headed: *Wasted energies.* He told himself sadly enough that, with or without his intervention, the good people of Arc-sur-Loire would continue to be good in a way which precluded all progress, and that this notwithstanding, he must continue to walk beside them, calling to them every now and again with an appeal as monotonous as the call of a cow-herd to his oxen. By degrees he must fatally sink to their level. What had he to occupy him to-day, for instance, while all the thoughts of his hearers would be concentrated on the important subject of carrying and garnering the corn? To settle some minor details of administration, casual ones that he found particularly odious. He shrugged his shoulders, and again took up his breviary.

"*Monsieur le Curé*—a letter for you," repeated Ursula, passing into the arbour this time.

"A letter?"

The hour for the postman to pass was long over; epistolary correspondence with their pastor had never obtained among the parishioners of Arc-sur-Loire.

"Give it me," said he, quite surprised.

Something strange was happening to him, something out of the common.

"Is it possible? They have sent from *La Prée* for me."

"*La Prée!*" echoed Ursula. Those heretics! What an event, indeed!"

"I want to know . . . Say that I will go, as they wish it; or rather, no, do not send the messenger away. I am ready to go with him."

He stood up as he spoke, rather agitated, and crossing the garden in a few strides, re-read the letter, a note of two lines written in a trembling hand, from which he learnt nothing more than that a sick and unhappy person wished to see him without delay.

That was enough for the Abbé Fulgence. He snatched up his hat and stick, and without a question, followed the little peasant who had come to seek him; while Ursula, standing on the threshold of the presbytery, followed with her eyes the tall figure that stood out from the blinding glare of the white dust, as it passed along the high road.

"What can they want with him?" she asked herself, with a vague sensation of uneasiness.

II.

La Prée, an important domain situated far from the village, in the midst of a rich zone of cornfields and vineyards, was the last stronghold of Protestantism where it had once been so powerful. The cognomen of its owners, evidently derived from a significant nickname, recalled the old times of nocturnal preachings, and the popular belief in the supernatural powers that protected them. The family of Le Huguet had inhabited the country from generation to generation since those remote times, isolated in a manner which would have been explicable in that bygone period of warlike persecution, but singular in this present day of avowed liberty of creed. This isolation (which nowise precluded public esteem, and the sort of respect due to a higher status, more or less dependent on a person's means) was certainly owed to the peculiar attitude of this nest of Huguenots, living, as it were, under the ban of old custom, and in the shade of hereditary memories.

Not that the Le Huguets made any display of the faith they alone adhered to; indeed, they were generally considered to belong to no sort of religion, because they attended no place of worship. They lived at a great distance from the principal town of their department, and there only could they have met with a minister of their own faith; so they limited their calls on his services to the great solemnities of life, marriage, baptism, or burial, refraining at all other times from every external form of worship.

"He is like ourselves—nothing at all," asserted the two or three Freethinkers, designated " Reds " by the population of Arc-sur-Loire, when they mentioned François Le Huguet.

But they were mistaken. The master of *La Prée*, although no longer called upon to attend secret preachings, would sooner have suffered at the stake or in exile, like his forefathers, than have denied by word or deed the faith to which he clung, as to his life's blood, by a dogged instinct. He was himself the priest of his own home, and every evening he read, for the edification of his wife and children, a few verses from an ancient yellow-leaved, well-worn edition of the Bible, which bore the date of 1588. This Bible was a sacred relic. It represented the altar at which the household knelt, the foundation-stone of a house where everything told of its presence, for surely never did outer walls and all they enclosed differ more entirely from their surroundings. The other farms, from the poorest to the richest, had an unvarying family likeness, with their hedge of brambles the more or less picturesque disorder of the yard, with its agricultural implements, its dung-heaps, its free and untrammelled poultry and pigs, and its children, all unwashed until the Sabbath day. The inhabitants of the *Orléanais* are all comparatively clean. But at *La Prée*, amidst the cold symmetry of those whitewashed walls, within those gates, painted so crude a green, one might fancy oneself in Switzerland or in Holland.

Every one was conscious, after the the first steps across the yard devoted to the business of the farm, that here was a difference which must extend from external objects to the character of the inhabitants. Vast stores of manure filled the pits *ad hoc*, without a blade of straw passing their stone edges; the ground was carefully weeded, and the animals shut up in their respective quarters, which formed scrupulously neat geometrical squares. The dairy produce of *La Prée*, whether butter or cheese, had its special market value, the servants who had lived there were in request because they were accredited with order, industry, and general good conduct. The master passed for a man of austere and taciturn disposition. He associated as little as possible with the villagers, neither did he make any advances to the neighbouring townspeople, although his position as a great agriculturist entitled him to rank with them. Notwithstanding his horny hands and brusque manners, his very reserve imposed respect; he was not easily approached or understood, and none appeared to be at ease with him. Although strictly honest in his dealings, and chary of his words, he never lost sight of his own interest. His every action indicated a fund of sagacity, rigorous justice, and secret distrust. The truth is, that he was always on the defensive, standing as he did alone against the world, regarded as an Anti-christ by the pious, and as an alien by the mass of the population, which formed, so to speak, one huge family in the bonds of continued intermarriage; while for the last century no Le Huguet had made any alliance with his neighbours. Madame Le Huguet was of Teuton extraction, stout and languid; she reminded one of Holbein's matrons. A silent country *bourgeoise*, entirely given up to the direction of her household, she seemed almost to have fallen into double bondage to husband and children. The latter was indeed a light and pleasant one, and borne most willingly by an adoring mother.　They were three girls, real young ladies, who had been educated up to the age of fifteen at a boarding school in the town, where they had learnt to play the piano.　Novels came for them by post from the circulating library; all this was food for no small amount of gossip.

They were decidedly original—very proud, and yet by no means vain, it was said.　A certain puritan simplicity in their dress prevented the vulgar from perceiving their innate elegance.　Shod in a manner to defy the worst roads, generally clad in dark woollen materials, their heads covered with little mannish hats, they were outwardly not unlike English girls, *de jeunes misses*.　The eldest was already married to a wealthy tanner of Touraine, and there was a marked difference of age between the two younger ones.　Little Suzette might often be seen driving a be-ribboned donkey in a tiny English cart all about the country.　She responded to the salutations that were addressed to her with a shyness which was infinitely prepossessing, and was, like a true Le Huguet, of few words.

As to the other sister, Mademoiselle Simone, she had been invisible for months, and was known to be ill. The doctor went to *La Prée* regularly twice a week, .and sometimes he was sent for oftener. For the last eight days his *cabriolet* had been seen to pass that way every day.

"It was such a pity! such a pretty girl! the flower of the flock—a queenly figure! And what a colour she had when she came home from school!" But she had fallen into consumption by slow degrees, and soon perhaps she would rejoin those dead and gone Le Huguets who rested under the large white stone at the farther end of the burying ground, isolated in death as they had been in life, and even there a mark for the tongue of scandal. The thick turf of God's acre was planted with many crosses, large and small. "Those people at *La Prée* must be downright heathen to renounce this symbol." "Christians ? oh, dear, no ! They called themselves Christians, but nobody believed it." "Hadn't they told Catherine, the girl who tended their poultry, who had offered to make a *neuvaine* to the Holy Virgin for *Mademoiselle*, that they did not tolerate such superstitions under their roof ?" Meanwhile they were unhappy.

The father unbent less than ever. No complaint escaped his close-shut lips, but there was a heartbroken ring in his harsh voice when the imperious mouth had to frame an order; the mother had suddenly aged ten years, and little Suzette, when you asked her how her sister was, answered, while she struggled to restrain her tears,—

"She is no better."

The *Curé*, like every one else, had heard of this illness. His first thought was naturally of the stricken one. But what did she want of him ? His brain began to work. Was it a last mysterious request, or a confession, perhaps,—one of those confessions which prove the human as well as the divine need of the sacrament of repentance, and which is said to have thrust certain Protestants, especially women, into the confessional, where they can be heard if not absolved? If it were more than that, if grace had touched this erring soul, and melted away its clouds! if he were to have the signal glory of leading it back to God! The apostle's heart within him swelled with hope.

Once he turned to speak to the little boy who was guiding him, and whose feet tripped lightly over the stubble, for as the harvests were over this side of the farm they went across the fields.

"What is thy name?"

"Baptistin."

"Thou art in service at *La Prée?*"

"No, indeed; I came with my mother from the hamlet of Guignes to glean. Madame Le Huguet, who knows me by sight, gave me the scrap of paper and told me not to tell any one where I was taking it to."

"Some one is ill at the farm?"

"Yes, one of the young ladies has been ill for a long time."

"And she wishes to see me?"

"I don't know; I did as I was told. I met Monsieur Le Huguet, who was overlooking the reapers over by Petite-croix. He asked me where I was running to so fast. I said I was going to the town to fetch some stores. If he knew that I told a story, I should get a good shaking. He hates lies worse than anything, I think, Monsieur le Huguet does; he'd rather be robbed, I think, and yet——"

The boy stopped short and reddened up to his eyes. He remembered the severest punishment which had ever fallen to his lot, when one day the owner of *La Prée* had discovered him in his orchard in the act of eating his apples.

III.

Monsieur le Curé, led by little Baptistin, walked a long way. If the village of Arc, properly speaking, is composed of but a few houses perched high on the hill that overlooks the Loire and its great sandy curves, the parish of Arc-sur-Loire extends far into the plain, and the Le Huguet property stood at its uttermost limit. The sun was already sinking, when, in the turn of the road which they had reached, the long green fence revealed itself, surrounding a compact group of simple one-storeyed buildings, devoid of any character and staringly white-washed.

A woman was waiting on the threshold, and looking impatiently from right to left. She was a little woman, short and stout, whose black silk apron peeped out from under the print skirt which had been partly tucked up to preserve it. Her silver grey hair was swathed in folds of muslin, and from her waist there hung a large bunch of housewife's keys. As he came nearer to her, the *Abbé* perceived that her face bore traces of recent tears. It was Madame le Huguet. After dismissing little Baptistin, she said:

"Sir, I must confess to you that you are not here by my desire, still less by the wish of my husband, who must never hear of your visit. I have managed for the moment to get every one out of the way. Enter quickly."

"Still, madam," replied the astonished *Curé*, "this letter is in your handwriting, I suppose?"

Madame Le Huguet dried her eyes. She was evidently agitated.

"I had to consent! . . . I know that I am wrong; . . . but when you are entreated by one in the jaws of death, what can you do? How could I, her mother, hold out to the end? Como in quickly, I tell you. . . . He is the man to kill you if he guessed . . ."

She led him across the courtyard, and round a corner of the house. From this side a small wooden outside staircase led to the first floor. Madame le Huguet, still preceding the *Curé*, drew a key from her pocket, and after looking once more timidly and furtively around her, opened the little door at the head of the stair, and then asked the young priest to wait in the linen-closet, littered all over, as she apologetically remarked, with linen from the recent wash. From the next room, when she entered, there came a weak cry, almost immediately repressed; then a rustling of stuffs and an interchange of rapid whispering before Madame le Huguet returned, only to disappear again, after showing the Abbé into the bedroom.

He found himself in a large apartment, wherein half-closed shutters made a twilight of the light that passed through them. The window, that overlooked the courtyard from between the folds of its curtains, had been hermetically closed; it was from the garden that the odours of carnations and of lavender, too pungent for the nerves of an invalid, were wafted into the room. At sight of the *Curé*, some one lying on the wide chintz-hung bed made a feeble effort to rise into an upright posture. This he did not notice at first, as he had turned round to see if his introductress had followed him. No; the door was shut, and he was alone, alone with the pale apparition, whose whiteness blended with the white of the bed-linen in the gloom of the alcove. But soon the eyes of the Abbé Fulgence grew accustomed to the darkness and distinguished a woman, a young woman with large eyes dulled by the deep circles round them, and with a waxen skin. The only life in her whole being seemed to cling to her golden-brown hair; it had been plaited in two heavy, shining plaits, which laid out on the bed by her side, and formed a frame to her face and figure. But for them, she might have been a statue on a tomb.

Yet, as the priest approached her, a hectic flush coloured the cheek bones, and the hands tightly clasped together loosened themselves, as she murmured:

"I thank you!"

Then only did he recognise, or rather recall, a face of which this was but the shadow, and that he had often passed it without having so much as asked: Who is she? That face, forgotten until this moment appeared to him by a rapid process of mental evocation more distinctly than it had ever done in reality; indeed, he was surprised—never having noticed it before or thought of it since—to remember it so vividly all at once.

"You are Mademoiselle Simone?" said he, taking his seat by the bedside with an affectionate familiarity habitual to him in the sick room, without waiting to be invited to do so.

She smiled a wan smile at her name, and answered:

"I am nothing now, nothing but a girl who is going to die."

"Who knows? There is God to lean upon, and to His power there is no limit. It is you, my child, who have sent for me?"

A brighter burning red, painful to see, lighted up the hollow cheeks, and she turned her head aside and buried it in the pillow with a strange confusion. Then a hoarse cough overcame her and shook her emaciated shoulders. The cough, the almost transparent thinness, other fatal signs, told their tale but too clearly to the *Curé*. Consumption in its last stage had worn the unhappy creature's life away, leaving to the approaching terrors of death but a frail shell, in itself almost ethereal. As she lay back panting, with moist brow, she fixed her eyes on his face with an expression which would have embarrassed him had he not often encountered a like intensity in the eyes of the dying, an intensity by which they seem to appropriate with their latest energies all that they are about to lose for ever.

The clock on the mantelpiece struck the minutes solemnly, and another muffled sound, like the despairing thud of a breaking heart, mingled with its regular ticking. For a long while it filled the silent room. The Abbé waited: at last he attempted to break through this timidity or indecision.

"What can I do for you?"

"Oh!" she said, "you have already done more than I dared to hope in coming here."

"Charity is enjoined upon me by the God whom I serve," replied the young priest simply. "It is my duty to hasten whither I am called, without even trying to fathom the motives of those who suffer and call upon me."

She moaned as if he had wounded her. A sad echo repeated:

"Your duty!"

And then there was once more silence for some minutes.

"Your duty," she began again, "will doubtless prevent your returning here. What does it matter? . . . You will know, you will have read, . . . for I could not possibly speak . . . I dare not, . . . I should be ashamed. . . ."

Once more the little blood left to her rushed to her brow, lighting up her dark, tearful eyes. She succeeded in raising herself, but with a contraction of the features which betokened so much suffering that the priest involuntarily drew nearer to help her, but she put up her arm as if in alarm; and whilst she kept him at a distance, searched for something under her pillow.

"You promise to read it?" she said, as she handed him a thin book bound in shagreen. A little key hung from its clasp. "It is a confession, my dying confession, you see. There ought to be indulgence for that."

In taking the book from her his hand touched her slender fingers, which thrilled at the contact like the leaves of a sensitive plant.

"Ah!" she sobbed, "when you know, you will not come back."

"Nothing shall prevent me from coming here to minister to you," he replied, moved by a profound pity.

Suddenly there was light on her despairing face.

"Do not doubt the mercy of the All-Merciful."

"I only doubt your mercy," she broke in, and would have added something more, when Madame Le Huguet, opening the door without showing herself, said, in a tone of anguish:

"This is the hour when thy father returns from the fields."

"*Adieu!*" murmured the sick girl.

"*Au revoir!*" replied the *Curé*.

He perceived that she made a vague effort to shake hands with him, and remembering that his

Divine Master would not have refused to touch the hand of the Canaanite, he took this poor hand in his with the awkwardness of a man who has never permitted himself such familiarities. His surprise to find his own hand drawn towards trembling lips which printed a pressure as of fire upon it, partook of dismay. A moment later he was on the highroad, without knowing how he had left the room.

Then the idea that the poor girl's mind was wandering, that she was delirious, came to him, and he accepted it; this spontaneous gesture was surely due to fever. The whole adventure seemed so strange to him that had it not been for the locked book in his pocket, inviting him to read, to know. . . . From one minute to another, as he walked, his curiosity grew stronger. At last he could withstand it no longer, and, sitting down by the way under a group of trees that overhung a grassy mound, he plunged into the reading of the book which was to give him the key of the mystery. It was the tranquil hour immediately after sunset; the sonorous air rang with the distant song of the reapers.

At that moment, François Le Huguet passed, with his hands crossed behind his back and his head bent down, to avoid raising his hat, and the priest started like a burglar caught in the act.

IV.

Was it the sudden apparition of this father who was to be kept in the dark, or because the steel clasp was difficult to open, that he felt a vague and passing fear of committing an indelicate act, and almost feared to encounter the secret which had been voluntarily placed in his hands? It was a confession, she had said. But this confession of a Protestant was an extraordinary action, to which he had perhaps not been justified in lending himself without first ascertaining in what spirit it had been made. To gain time, and also to reassure himself, he first glanced at the earliest, somewhat faded pages; a line across them in pencil showed that they were of no importance or account: the ordinary young girl's diary, insignificant and monotonous. The writing was careful and regular: a pretty small handwriting, with capital letters of an elaborate design, relieved by bold round hand for details of paramount interest. Under each date a few lines accounted for the daily employment of time since the first day of school-life, class triumphs, detailed accounts of great functions, a competition, a distribution of prizes; and effusions inspired by the naïve passion of childish friendships ran like a thread through all the artless recital of the small joys and sorrows—the joys and sorrows of an age when everything is exaggerated by vivacity of imagination, warmth of heart, and the shallowness of emotion.

These joys and these sorrows seemed in Simone's case to be abnormally out of proportion to the events which gave rise to them. Besides, there seemed to have been shocks and contrasts in her existence which could not have produced any very healthy effect on the development of a character whose chief elements appeared to have consisted in a remarkable pride and a perilous tendency to dreaminess. A young lady at the boarding school, Simone le Huguet became once more a peasant girl during her holidays at home, and this dual life was for some time described with a lightness of heart which betrayed a happy faculty for keen enjoyment. By degrees, however, the young lady's tastes predominated, the harvest and haymakings gave her less pleasure; the homestead, overflowing as it was with comfort, appeared to her to be wanting in common necessaries. After her last, especially brilliant year of study, she had claimed a wardrobe with a mirror in it, and a rosewood writing-table for her room, as a reward.

Her elder sister Julie, who had had the same

education, was much less exacting, and laughed a little at her aspirations. Julie, although she had no love of the country, did not form any too ambitious projects. She would have been satisfied to marry a tradesman, and to have dwelt in a small town. Simone did not think of marriage, but her fancy spread open wings of boundless reach towards a vague, perhaps inaccessible, and certainly limitless future. Her style here became more inflated, and acquired an emphatic, romantic ring. The conquest of a diploma had inspired her with the desire to become a governess, to follow in the wake of a rich and noble foreign family, and to see the world; a means of escape from the commonplaces she foresaw, of flight towards the unknown. Her parents opposed this wish. She did not need to gain her living; she was rich, thank goodness! She would marry prosperously! Then came the return to *La Prée*, the weariness of it, and the veiled lamentations, the injustice of which she was the first to recognise. For her father adored her, notwithstanding his severity, and her mother granted her every wish except the liberty to seek elsewhere a happiness she was unlikely to attain. But without it how profound and intolerable was the emptiness of her existence. . . . Bred from her birth upwards to country pursuits, she could not feel their poetry; it was all too simple. She dreamt of mountains and seas that she had never beheld, and in the midst of waving cornfields, of hills bristling with vine-hung poles. Heart and brain were pure, but full of dreams of knowledge and conquest. She would have revelled in the unforeseen, yet nothing ever came to pass, no new face, no incident which differed from those of every day came to change the current of her thoughts. The people about her, even her sister who had nothing but marriage in view, and who was already disposed to accept the first suitable *parti*, were all too inferior to her. At first there had been a lively correspondence with several of her old schoolfellows, and then it had come to a standstill, either through her own fault, or that of her friends, who had no longer any interests in common with her, and who, by telling her of what was never to be her lot, only increased her dissatisfaction. One who stood higher than herself in the social scale was passing her honeymoon on the shores of an Italian lake; another less favoured by fortune was making a living by her talent. She would fain have been a real lady like the former, or absolute mistress of her actions like the latter. Why had she no equals? Her books soon became her only resource; but in immersing herself in them she only called new wants and the thirst of a higher ideal into being. This led her to a hatred of the education she had received, the culture which cut her off from her peaceful, well-fed surroundings. Surrounded by material abundance, she despised her commonplace comforts, and was, so to speak, dying of spiritual hunger. Music, which she adored, while far from excelling in it, and to

which she had owed so many delightful hours at
school, no longer consoled her; her piano was an
exile in the large rustic house, where the only listeners
were the swineherds and poultry-maids, who would
have listened to any other noise with the same open
round eyes and wide-open mouth.

"What is the good of it?" repeated Simone to
herself, as she shut the instrument to which her
father bore a grudge for having cost so much, and
renouncing the studies which, instead of calming her
secret irritation had excited it, laid down her arms,
and let the life about her become gradually narrower
and more oppressive.

"What was the good of it?" . . . This query
reappeared with or without commentary on every
page of the journal. Then she had apparently
wearied of the journal itself, for many pages were
left blank, and a long time elapsed before she again
wrote on the white space, which expressed better
than any words could have done the extent of her

discouragement and *ennui*. Nothing . . . she had nothing more to say?

"Poor child!" thought the priest with a rush of sympathy. He, too, had uttered the sad words, "Of what avail?" when he compared his aspirations to his task. But the consciousness of duty accomplished, duty so humble that it was perhaps of greater merit, had compensated him, whilst this young girl seemed never to have given aught to God who takes count of our ordeals; here and there His name showed in a hasty note, or in a desperate appeal. This was not piety such as the Abbé Fulgence understood it, the piety which leads a tried soul to the altar's step, which confides it to the tender hands of that Virgin Mediator whom no Protestant implores.

"Poor child!" he repeated to himself, "had it but been given to her to kneel in a church, had she but submitted to an enlightened yoke, had the true faith been hers, she could have borne her lot. She has divined the truth late, but still she has divined it, seeing that she calls me to her aid!

Just at that moment the wind blew a loose page from the middle of the book on to the ground. He picked it up and grew pale as he read:

"How did I begin to love so madly a man condemned to celibacy by irrevocable vows, a Catholic priest, the one being in the world against whom I have been armed since my birth, whose superstitions used to be abhorrent to me? . . . I have thought so much about it that now I cannot help understanding it. To begin with, it was not a priest I saw in him that day, but a man —young, handsome, and intrepid—in the voluntary accomplishment of an heroic action which had nothing to do with his calling. Besides, he was the only person here whose face, mind, and character could possibly make any impression on me. . . . He was as unlike, more unlike the others, than myself, and after all what love, worthy the name, was ever turned from its course by the word 'Impossible'? I have cursed the obstacle, I have shattered myself against it, I am dying of it. . . . ."

The *Abbé* Fulgence suddenly closed the book and started to his feet, as if in alarm. Had he seen a sacrilegious hand seize the consecrated cup, his indignation could not have been stronger.

"Miserable woman!" he thought. "Miserable? She was right, I can do nothing for her—I must not even read her confession to the bitter end. May God have mercy on her!"

No merely human sentiment mingled in the young priest's mind with the horror of this profanation. His brow was clouded with the righteous anger of an offended archangel; but this wrath was in itself so like suffering that Ursula cried out when she saw him enter the presbytery:

"Good Heavens—what has happened to you, *Monsieur le Curé?* Can you be ill? You are as white as a sheet."

"I am only a little tired, my good Ursula; do not be anxious," he answered, as he passed on to his room, without appearing to notice that the table was laid.

"Really there is neither rhyme nor reason in dining at this late hour! Don't keep your soup waiting any longer, *Monsieur le Curé*. I had hard work to keep it from burning."

"Thank you; I shall not dine. Leave me alone. All I want is a little rest; it's useless to insist, Ursula."

And the Abbé Fulgence shut himself in and bolted his door, while his *gouvernante* raised her hands to Heaven in her efforts to guess what had happened in that nest of heretics at *La Prée* to put him into such a state. She was still more puzzled in the morning when she discovered that her master had not gone to bed that night, and that his candle had burned down to the socket. For all that, at six o'clock he went to say Mass with his usual serenity.

V.

Like those fearsome souls who, to allay their own cowardice, force themselves to face the phantom the sight of which has nearly put them to flight, thus to assure themselves of their own folly, the Abbé Fulgence on his return to his own home had argued with himself, probed the danger, and finally found himself strong enough to vanquish it. After all, what justified so violent an alarm? Did he feel any secret weakness in his innermost soul? Without hesitation he could answer—No. That woman already dead to this world was surely not redoubtable; prudence had nought to do with the sentiment which caused him to avoid her. And why so severe to the poor misguided one? Was she really criminal? In her Protestant eyes he was not the Anointed of the Lord, he was not clothed with the indelible sanctity which should silence profane thoughts; he was only a man like other men—she had said so. He might as well punish a stranger for not comprehending our language, albeit unknown to him.

All at once it struck the Abbé Fulgence that his conduct was absurd and cowardly; it appeared to him that it was his duty to battle with the evil spirit, or at least to decide on further investigation whether the combat was possible. Resolutely he reopened the book which had shocked him so profoundly, and read without further intermittence from the first to the last line. The journal was taken up again towards the autumn of the year he had been installed in his parish of Arc-sur-Loire.

"*A Fire.*—The whole farm of Chesnayes, near the village, has been devoured by fire. We saw the sky aflame for a great distance, enormous columns of red smoke arose out of the night from behind the trees. Father had the horse put to, to hasten to the spot; I insisted on accompanying him, attracted, fascinated by the frightful spectacle. . . . All the village was abroad, dogs howled, the tocsin rang. . . . A confused and sinister noise of hurried steps, clamour, lamentation. . . . The engines worked badly, the buckets of water carried from hand to hand came too slowly. Whilst this inefficient aid was being organized the flames raged, devouring the walls, flashing through the door, bursting through the roof. In the height of the danger he appeared to me! In a ringing voice he gave orders to the frightened, helpless people, and with splendid coolness he seemed to accomplish more than all the others put together. What a crash! Part of the roof has just fallen in. He is buried, I think, under the ruins. . . . But no; behold him a little further on, mounting a ladder, whilst around him heaps of straw and grain of every kind hiss as they send up long jets of flame. The farmer's family only think of saving their cattle and their furniture. . . . All at once a childish voice sends forth a piteous appeal. All eyes turn towards the loophole of a barn, over the cattle yard. An orphan from the charity school, brought up in the house, is there, a prisoner of the flames. No one has thought of him, but he awakes—too late. Fire blocks the way. Lost! . . . he is lost! . . . and they turn away not to see the end. After all, the existence of this unhappy child whom no one claims is not of much importance. There are other losses, serious, material ones. . . . O cowards! cowards! One alone devotes himself. . . . Even now I can see him plunge into the fiery furnace. Now they all say, 'They are both lost.' My heart stops beating. But soon he reappears, with singed hair and garments and blackened face, carrying the inanimate child in his arms. Hurrah! hurrah! I ask, 'Who is this intrepid man?' And they answer, 'It is the new *Curé.*'"

The Abbé Fulgence had often recalled that night, to thank God who had permitted him to save the life of a human being. But it seemed to him that the recital of his achievement was a singularly exaggerated one.

"Really," he said to himself with a sarcastic smile, "I should be justified in thinking myself a hero, because I helped to make the chain in a fire. What big words! How much she must have needed enthusiasm for some one or something!"

Still, he knew what popularity his conduct at the Chesnayes fire had won for him in the district, a popularity of which he had guaged the emptiness, for it lasted just as long as the memory of a benefit conferred usually lasts, a few weeks. But Simone's journal dwelt lovingly on this period of popularity, and prolonged it. It was evident that she sought every opportunity of speaking of him, that she studied his every act, and gloried in hearing that he was the most generous, the most affable, and the most learned among men. Each of their accidental meetings was inscribed, "This morning he passed me on the highroad.

He immediately bowed to me with grave politeness. The old *Curé* did not bow to us. He spoke of us everywhere as the scourge of the parish, as impious, accursed beings. There is nothing fanatical about this one. But being what he is, by what aberration can he have been led to join a clergy which condemns all light, which excommunicates all liberty of thought? I like to think of him as he might have been, with that black livery stripped from him, free, with the right to love a woman who would have adored him. What blindness can have led him on to suicide? A love trouble perhaps. Would that be possible? Who would not have loved him?"

"Poor insane creature!" thought the Abbé Fulgence; "how far she is from the truth, how she raves!"

And he remembered how easy had been the road from the school to the great seminary. He had never hesitated as to his vocation. The instinct of faith and obedience was so natural to him that he was unconscious of any merit in the entire sacrifice of his personality. Secure on the immutable Rock of Theology, he could defy error. What enlightenment could she conceive of? He knew himself to be, by the grace of God, the dispenser of truth. Why had her search not led her even to the Shrine? His teaching might have brought her conviction, the erring tortured mind would, in listening to his words, have risen from the servant to the master. She *had* been there, she had entered the nave from curiosity, from a longing to see him. Hidden behind a pillar, she had witnessed the ceremonial of a creed from which her reason repelled her, and it had not been borne in upon her that an insurmountable obstacle hedged in this young saint from all human affections, although she beheld him isolated, glorified in the hieratic vestment of an older time, through the incense clouds of the divine rites.

"Doubtless, he is eloquent," she continued, "and full of faith, but I have listened to words no less efficacious from the lips of ministers who were just men in my sight, and yet had not broken with human nature, who, while they cared for souls, did not repudiate the joys of family life, cherishing their wives and educating their children. How can one believe in the merit of sterile, and perhaps desolate celibacy?" It was evident that while she looked upon it as an error, this sublime folly, this superhuman idealism did but excite the enthusiasm of Simone. She compared ordinary mankind to the exceptional being estranged from all earthly ties, with supreme contempt for this country lawyer or for that rich neighbouring miller who had made her an offer of marriage. How coarse they were! And how ugly and vulgar! With the record of every offer there reappeared the portrait of the Abbé Fulgence, and he, who held for beauty the passionate contempt of an early

Christian, felt tempted to mutilate his own face, rather than that face with which he had never concerned himself should prove for him, as if he were a woman, a stumbling-block, a danger! "Handsome? was it possible that he was handsome? . . . what could it mean?"

"Lord," he murmured, as he read on with a mingling of embarrassment and contempt, "hasten the day of my old age and all it brings with it!"

The growth and development of such a love, unfed as it had been, attested the want of balance of the feminine nature, where fancy has unbridled sway. So might a microscopic germ fall by chance into soil only too ready to receive it, germinate into a living plant, and end by becoming the poisonous tree whose indestructible roots and sinister shade destroy all surrounding vegetation.

This life in love passed through a phase of asceticism. Of her own free will Simone imposed every kind of privation and sacrifice upon herself, so that she might raise herself a little towards those moral heights where dwelt the unconscious object of her affections; she devoted herself to visiting the poor and nursing the sick, in the hope, occasionally realized, of meeting him in the presence of those sufferings they both endeavoured to alleviate, and which she thought they would together have been better able to cure. Her father said to her:

"Now you are becoming so perfect, we must make a minister's wife of you."

The effect of solitude, which Julie's marriage had intensified was to turn her chimera into a monomania, which took the form of projected letters, alternately burning or timorous, although they never came to anything. One, however, was thrown into the post-box one day that her father had taken her with him to town. No sooner was the letter posted than she would have given anything to have it back. If he guessed, she should die of shame !

Alas ! two days later she met him just outside the village on his way to visit his parishioners. She felt ready to swoon, so persuaded was she that his glance would flash upon her like a burning brand. The look, before which she had trembled in imagination, had not even been accorded to her. He had not even perceived her, so absorbed was he in his thoughts. What was he thinking of? Of her letter perhaps. Had he not drawn it out of his pocket to read it as he walked? No, a thousand times no ! what he was reading so intently was his breviary.

What matter? the first step had been made, she resolved to continue, resolved to reach him, despite the triple wall of the sanctuary, resolved that nothing should keep her back . . . Oh, how the regular schoolgirl's handwriting, so monotonously even at first, had changed ! Now it was impatience, anguish, passion which guided her hand, now supplicating, now ready for menace. She would see him, would find a pretext for speaking to him. But what pretext? In vain she sought for one; she could find none. She was still seeking and still hopeless, when on a certain evening a blind desperate influence had drawn her to the vicarage. As if to further her design, the garden gate was open, the kitchen-door too, and Ursula absent. She had crossed the little dining-room in all its monastic simplicity, trembling lest she should meet him she longed to see. She pushed open the first door she came to, the *Abbé's* room; his narrow bed, a deal table, a crucifix, some rushbottomed chairs, on the walls many shelves crowded with books, and on the bare table a forgotten rosary. She seized upon this amulet the use of which she was ignorant of, but which he must have touched, then snatching a rose from her bodice where it had lain fading since the morning had left it in its place.

A sound of steps in the next room . . . she had fled.

Between the lines the Abbé Fulgence could read his own almost forgotten memories. He remembered shrugging his shoulders whilst he burnt the anonymous letter, and the disappearance of the rosary he had sought for in vain for some time. As for the flower, he had not noticed it, it had had no meaning for him. All that was rather Ursula's fault, who too often went out to gossip with her neighbours, leaving the door open. Altogether, these trifling details made little impression upon him. On the other hand, he pitied the hidden drama of which this soul was the stage.

Alas! why, had not such an explosion of enthusiasm and love had God for its object? And once more he persuaded himself that he, the Abbé Fulgence, had been but a pretext. Is it not a law that the empty, neglected heart must attach itself to something? . . . especially a woman's heart, which cannot be compensated by intellectual gifts. Little girls have been known in the absence of a real object to fall in love with the hero of a novel, or even, when debarred from the complicity of a novel, with a phantom created by their own imagination, and which fancy they believe they recognise in the features of the first passer-by. He had been in the way. In fact what Simone loved in him was virtue, courage, all the perfections her own will had endowed him with. She had lost her way in the search for her ideal. Perhaps she but needed to be led back into the right way, the way which leads to God. Doubtless, like a true daughter of Eve, she had shown herself irritated by obstacles as well as tempted by forbidden fruit, but her purity had never failed her. That refined instinct had clung to her until the very gates of death, where the mortal part of her being had perished, worn out by fruitless waiting, undermined by vain dreams never to be realized. Ill as she was, she concealed this suffering, of which she alone knew the source, as if it were a crime. Her parents had been alarmed to see her waste away under their eyes for lack of sleep and appetite. The doctor they called in could make nothing of her; he could only perceive the external symptoms of the fatal passion which was wearing her life away. A nervous child, . . . that was all. Nerves gave you the fever, nerves make you cough. But the cough had become obstinate and tenacious, and the mysterious malady which betrays itself in those attacked by it in a gradual lessening of the vital forces, already deserved the expressive name of consumption, which covers so many causes. She had kept her own counsel so long; but at last, mastered by desire stronger than death, so strong that it took the place of thought and reason in her brain, she had sobbed out on her mother's bosom the secret it had needed all her pride to conceal. To see him from whom she was farther apart than ever, because she could no longer leave the house, she needed an accomplice; she trusted in maternal pity. For a long time Madame Le Huguet in despair had felt it her duty to resist; at last, when she saw how nearly extinguished was the fragile lamp she would have given her own life to rekindle, she had forgotten all her prudence. How could she bear to cull a supreme reproach, from the dying lips of her child, with her last farewell? Thus had it come to pass that the *Curé* of Arc had been summoned, as he surmised, although this last struggle had been unchronicled, the hand which had filled these mad burning, desperate pages, having for months past lost the power of writing.

After he had read, reflected and meditated during a long vigil, he closed the book, shook his head, and, at last, said out loud, "I will return there."

The calmness with which he uttered these words, words she prayed for with all the power of her will, would have fallen like an icicle on the heart of Simone Le Huguet, had she but heard them.

VI.

On the afternoon of the same day, the Abbé Fulgence heard the short trot of a horse, and the easy movement of a light vehicle, coming behind him on the highroad. It was the doctor; and he waited, for he wished to speak with him. Soon the old white mare turned the corner on which his eyes were fixed. He continued his way in apparent indifference.

"A fine day, doctor!" he cried from afar; "weather which ought to cure sick people."

"Yes, if it didn't kill them," broke in the doctor, who had stopped his mare. "I can do no more at *La Prée*. Those people don't interest you, *Monsieur le Curé*. They are not your parishioners. But you must confess that it is cruel to lose a girl of twenty-three, who is fading away like a drooping rose, without being able to find out what wind blows its leaves away! The deuce, if I know! What is the use of thirty years of practice, if it only leaves one contempt for medicine which leaves so much in obscurity. She is dying of phthisis, that is all I know about it. A fine achievement, to name the ill which one is able neither to forestall nor cure."

"She is dying? Is she really dying? Is there no hope?" asked the *Curé* pensively.

He only wanted to know whether the bold step he contemplated was warranted by the extreme gravity of the circumstances.

"To-morrow all may be over, and yet this misery may last another week or more. Yesterday evening I thought she would not have lived till sunrise. She had the most frightful attack!—her mother spoke vaguely of some excitement;—so fragile, the least thing moves her, the least thing upsets her; a breath is enough. She vibrates like glass, she will break as easily, poor little girl!"

"Really, is there no hope?" repeated the *Curé*, with singular persistence.

"Yes, one—the hope of a speedy end, that would come upon her suddenly. Horrible, these struggles of youth and death! Now, I must be off to assure myself of the fact that the old farmer of Petites-Croix, who will be a hundred at Easter, is in perfect health. What an irony of fate! His children have long since wearied of tending him; they confine themselves to letting him live on dry crusts—and he lives. Others die in their springtime. Oh, your Providence plays many a pretty trick! I had to break it to the unhappy parents. They must have known it for months; but the unexpected rallies in these diseases are so deceptive. One is so ready to believe that in the fight for existence the patient will get the upper hand, so ready to believe what one wishes for most. The father, all through his anxiety, never guessed at anything worse than a weakness that could easily be counteracted. Now he comes to me for help; he offers me half of all he possesses in exchange for his daughter's life. Oh, if health could be bought, the rogue would beggar mankind! The mother says nothing; I think she can sorrow no more. Poor things, poor things! such grief makes one wish with all one's heart that science were a real power!"

The doctor tickled his mare with the end of his whip, and she set off at a smart trot, whilst the Abbé Fulgence turned his steps in the contrary direction towards *La Prée*. As he walked, he thought—with a certain repugnance he devised an awkward expedient, in case the master of the house should be in the way, a guardian of that green gate which no *Curé* had passed through before him. But he soon took heart of grace. There was no one in the courtyard; no one but Madame Le Huguet, who sat knitting on the stone bench, and who came forward to meet him as if she had expected him. Her expression seemed to him sadder, and more troubled than the day before. You might have taken her for a sleep-walker, moving, although passive, without any participation of her own will in her movements, and, indeed, she was not her own master, but the slave of a tyranny no mother may resist. Her daughter, who had for so long shut her heart to sympathy, who had been cold and silent for such a weary time, had opened her heart at last, had wept on her bosom, whilst she smothered her with caresses, thus placing the consolation of her last days (or its alternative despair) in her hands. Tortured, she had yielded, knowing that she did wrong, and that her cowardice would heap coals of fire on her head; she took for granted her husband's wrath, and the wrath of a more redoubtable judge, to whom, throughout the livelong day, she addressed her mute prayer:

"Lord, may the punishment be mine, mine alone, O Lord!"

Without speaking to the priest, without looking at him, she led the way, as she had done on the previous day, and returned to watch in the court-yard.

This time the windows were closed, and the blinds drawn; instead of the perfume of the carnations in the garden, a smell of ether pervaded the room. The Abbé read the fatal sign on the weary brow. He had done well to come.

"Simone!" he said in a whisper, for she did not open her eyes when he entered.

She awoke suddenly out of her torpor, stretched her arms, and would have spoken. A gleam of joy had transfigured her, a joy still doubtful of itself, a joy that was mingled with terror, but above all with gratitude, an infinite gratitude.

"Oh, how good you are!" she murmured at last; "how good you are!"

And because she did not find in the eyes bent upon her all she wished to find there:

"Yes, you are indeed good," she continued timidly, "not to quite despise me. That book, how I wished I could have had it back after I had given it to you! They say I was delirious all night, and that I cried out, 'Do not read!' My father told me of it, without understanding. Perhaps you have not read it, for you have come back."

"I have read—I do not despise you, I pity you," he answered, in a strong, deep voice, softened by the pity he felt.

"You pity me?" she repeated.

Then after a pause, as if she had expected something else,—

"That is all you have to say to me?"

"No; I have much besides to say to you, my child, my sister. I have come to talk to you, as we may talk, I who belong to God, and you who are going to His presence, of a love denied to us ou earth, but which may, if it be your will, live once more up there, where there is no death."

She listened to him leaning on her elbow, all her soul in her eyes; a shudder stirred the wasted limbs that were defined by the sheets as by a shroud.

"Simone!" he repeated.

Her name on his lips! she smiled iu an ecstasy which might have transfigured the daughter of Jairus in the hour of her resurrection.

"Simone, you have told me the tale of a poor child who sinned, unconscious of her sin, and who gave her life for the involuntary crime of loving a man whose vows prohibited even the best joys this world has to give, a man who would have sooner died than perjure himself. Such love is no ordinary love. It burns the soul, or purifies it; it leads either to Heaven or to Hell, there is no neutral ground, for it attains to either eternal separation or eternal reunion."

"Reunion!" sighed Simone.

"Yes," said the Abbé, his fine face aglow with profound emotion. "'Tis for you to choose; my Master is between us here below." He drew from his girdle a little wooden crucifix which never left him and placed it on the bed, an august witness of their communion. "He forbids me to listen to a word that may lead me astray from Him. But what is this transient world? Were I the poor girl whose tortures you have confided to me, I would not be satisfied with so transitory an union; I should aspire to eternal union; I should wish to meet him who, instead of being the means of my fall had striven to be a means of grace, in that realm where sin is not, where obstacles do not exist, where all is love and purity."

"How can I?" she stammered, deceived by the apostle's ardour that was so like passion,—that was in reality that strongest of passions, proselytism.

"Do you not know that the souls who meet again are those who in this world have held one faith, and the same hope for the next? There is yet time. Let me teach you; or rather abandon yourself to the celestial inspiration which warns you that by strange and devious ways, God is leading you to knowledge of Himself."

"If your belief were mine, should we meet again?" she asked.

"I promise you we should."

"You believe it? Do you really believe it?"

"I am sure of it!" he answered in a tone of conviction.

"Speak then!" she cried.

And he did speak with eloquent warmth; without effort he found words which could open the burning wounded heart to the sublime tenderness, the mystic delight, the unrivalled consolations of Catholicism.

She listened with all her might, only caring to hear his voice as long as possible, to keep him near her by any possible means. The wish he had expressed to meet her in another life sufficed to lend enchantment to her last hour. Time flew: for her in the joy of his beloved presence, for him in enthusiasm for the creed he had begun to teach her. Of a sudden they heard Monsieur Le Huguet in the garden, calling out:

"I am going up to see Simone." And his wife answering in evident agitation:

"Mind you don't; she is sleeping."

Then a few moments later the mother said to the priest:

"Take advantage of his back being turned; leave at once."

"But to-morrow," murmured Simone; "to-morrow!"

"Yes, to-morrow," replied the Abbé Fulgence.

And Madame Le Huguet, as if in spite of herself, repeated, "To-morrow!" Glad in her sorrow of the thread that bound her child to life, certain that to-morrow, by the sovereign virtue of that hope, she would still be with her.

VII.

Twice, thrice did the *Curé* of Arc return to *La Préc*. He chose an hour when the father was away; he crept with stealthy steps towards the little back door mysteriously left on the latch; his wiles and precautions were as endless and varying as those a lover would employ to deceive the most jealous of guardians. His own intentions and the state, daily more alarming, of her he called his catechumen, justified this conduct in his own eyes. No scruple arose to stay his hand in this struggle, waged, as he thought, against the demon of heresy. Saint Paul never entered a hero's palace, where he too went to convert a woman, with a better armed conscience or a more heroic resolve: the young priest's only regret was that he met with no greater peril.

All was but too easy, thanks to the mother's

complicity, but the interest of his work absorbed him body and soul; those were the best filled days of his life, for they furnished him with emotion, the food he had most hungered for. In the interval of his visits to Simone, he prepared irresistible arguments; he strove to place the principle of love in opposition to the principle of Protestantism in which she had been bred; he condensed the doctrine into a compact and substantial form, measured to the requirements of those short interviews that were so soon to be interrupted. Besides, it mattered little to expound the dogma or to thoroughly reveal its symbolism; he only asked for a rush of faith and confidence, one of those inspired moments which leave their mark on eternity. Was he gaining ground? How could he prove it to himself?

She raised no objection, but listened on in silence, apparently docile. Sometimes a big tear fell from between her closed eyelids, sometimes she would cast a despairing glance at the glass placed opposite her bed, the glass of the famous wardrobe mentioned in the book with the lock. If, while he discoursed to the Christian of heaven, the woman wept over her vanished beauty, he knew it not, he did not look at her, so intent was he on gaining an end from which nothing could distract him. He never remarked the funereal coquetry with which she draped herself in folds of snowy white to receive him. One day she said to him:

"I am no longer a woman, I'm a spectre."

"You are a soul," he replied, "a purified soul; that is why I come here."

And when she persisted, saying: "Since you have taken pity on me, since I see you every day, death, which has always frightened me, seems less terrible."

He replied with his old austerity, "Do not regret life; it had nothing to give you," thus sending her back in sad submission to the unknown strand where she might await him. She feared the dark passage through the valley of the shadow, and would fain have turned her thoughts away from it; and then she would revel jealously and exclusively in the certainty of living in the memory of a heart closed to every other human feeling; then again, so faint a consolation would not suffice her. Earthly thoughts and sensations kept their hold on the dying girl, hidden though they were from him who, in the fulness of his youth and strength, was more dead than herself to mundane impressions. One article, however, of this new faith enchanted her, she hailed it with rapture; it was the invisible link, the near communion between those who are no more and those who survive them, leaving to one power over the other—the power of influencing destiny.

She said to the priest: "You will think of me, you will speak to me in your prayers, and I shall never be away from you, I shall never leave you for a moment . . . nevermore——"

These words were the last which passed her lips.

VIII.

He had baptized her with her full consent. The true faith he thought had at last, after centuries of rebellion, reached one of that hardened tribe of heretics. It would be a great example, a subject of edification for the whole parish. One morning when the Abbé Fulgence was alone in the sacristy, offering up to heaven the glory of the triumph he had been permitted to achieve, the door was pushed violently open by a man that no one had ever before seen in church. He was a thick-set and vigorous old man, whose harsh expression was heightened by a beard of some days' growth. Those grey bristles on his bronzed face made him look singularly fierce. The small hollow eyes under his bushy eyebrows flashed bloodshot gleams; his fist trembled as he grasped a stick, whilst he stood right in front of the *Curé* and looked straight into his eyes.

"She belongs to you," he blurted out. "I leave her to you, come and fetch her. Yes; take her body, since you have stolen her soul. The crime will be none the greater. Thief! seducer! that is what you are; do you hear? When she left us, she told us that she died a Catholic—she, my daughter! Her mother has confessed all to me, her mother, who has been the go-between—for pity's sake, she says—for pity! I, in pity for her honour, for the honour of her people, in pity for her eternal soul,—I would sooner have shut the door of our family vault upon her before the time, and, armed with my gun, I would have mounted guard over it. But by my own people have I been betrayed! And my wife and daughter have conspired against me! they are as dead to me. Falsehood has entered into my gates in your track. For your sake an unhappy girl has denied her father and her faith. Under the pretext of turning her into a saint of your own making, you have wrought her damnation. Yes, damnation; for it was not to your God that she gave herself, 'twas to a man—to you! You—you were her god. If you did not know it, it was because you would not know it. The soul of my daughter is damned because she made unto herself an idol of flesh and blood. Now take away the rest."

He shook his stick and went away, without having allowed himself to be interrupted, without having deigned to listen to a word.

The Abbé saw him once more, seated in the court-yard at *La Prée*, motionless, with arms crossed and hat drawn down over his eyes, when he went, fol-lowed by a long procession of peasants chanting the psalms, to fetch the body which had been yielded up to him with a curse. This time he entered by the great door, which was thrown wide open. The mother sobbed, hidden in the curtains of the bed which had witnessed so long an agony; she did not raise her head. Little Suzette stood upright on the stair and looked on terrified out of her large black eyes—the eyes of Simone; those whom the father had called thieves carried the body away. And old Le Huguet, when the coffin was carried past him, did not stir from his seat in the sun; he seemed petrified. The white banner carried by the maidens waved over the green hedges at every turning in the road until it was out of sight; the distant voices melted away and died, until the melancholy, far-off sound of the bell tolling in the village was the only one to be heard.

The old Huguenot was still there, meditating with dry eye and clenched fist in the midst of the ruins of his fallen pride, on the first defection of which one of his race had given the example.

"To abjure!" he murmured, in the tone in which a soldier might have said, "To desert!"

The fanatic had forbidden his family and his ser-

vants to appear either in church or at the cemetery.
The crowd at Simone's funeral was all the greater.
The whole population of Arc-sur-Loire made it
the pretext of a religious demonstration; and, for
once, so far departed from its habitual parsimony
as to club together, the poorest giving his mite,
so that a beautiful stone cross on a corpse snatched
from the Protestant camp might recall the almost
miraculous conversion of a Le Huguet.

IX.

THE gravestone is blackened by many winters; the
farm of *La Prée* still maintains its old aspect of
hostile isolation and cold, symmetrical prosperity;
but for all these years no one has heard of the
Abbé Fulgence.

After the conquest which had done him so much
honour, every one noticed that he was not the same
man. Pale, sad, and ever preoccupied, was he
thinking of the father's fierce malediction, which

had fallen on him at the very steps of the altar? Or, was it that the intangible betrothed he had taken to himself for eternity returned too often to remind him of a tryst that alarmed his conscience? Who can say whether during those ever-lengthening hours of meditation spent in the arbour, where he had received the letter that summoned him to *Im Prée* for the first time, there did not pass between him and his breviary the girl who had said:

"I will never leave you more!"

Perhaps she appeared henceforward not in her shroud, wasted by prematurely hopeless passion, but young, beautiful, living—the Simone of the locked book. One evening Ursula saw her master throw into the fire, with a desperate gesture, as if he would burn a wizard's charm, a little book bound in black shagreen. This rite did not, however, give him back his ease of mind, or his resolute, militant humour. He had no longer faith in himself or in his vocation; thoughts possessed him which were not his own, but must have been those of Simone, instilled into him, whispered into his ear; the fine zeal which had once inspired him had worn itself out in the first excessive effort. Suddenly, that he might fly from the sort of indefinable remorse which tortured his cowed spirit, he asked to be sent to a smaller, more isolated parish than Arc-sur-Loire. His bishop granted a request which appeared to be dictated by profound humility. And the Abbé Fulgence was ere long to give a further proof of his renunciation of self and his terror of responsibility. He soon retired from active ministration. The rumour spread that he had entered one of those *chartreuses*, where the last fragment of human will is immolated, where in the strait bonds of an iron rule there is no room for wandering, no risk of mistaking evil for good. But where be walls high enough and strong enough to bar the way to memory, that ghost which can never be laid?

THE ETRUSCAN VASE.

(PROSPER MÉRIMÉE.)

Auguste Saint Clair was not popular in what is called society, chiefly because he did not choose to be agreeable except with people whom he cared for. These he would go out of his way to seek; as to the others, he kept out of their way. And Saint Clair was indolent and absent-minded. One evening, when he had just come from the opera, the Marquise A—— asked him how Mademoiselle Sontag had sung.

"Yes, madame," answered Saint Clair, with a sweet smile and with his thoughts leagues away. This absurd answer could not be attributed to shyness, for Saint Clair talked to the great, to great men, and even to women of fashion, with as much *aplomb* as to his equals. The marquise made up her mind that he was a prodigy of impertinence and conceit.

Madame B—— asked him to dine on a Monday. She talked to him a good deal, and he went home declaring that he had never met a more agreeable woman. Now it was the manner of this lady to collect good things among her friends for a month, and to fire them all off at home in one evening. Saint Clair met her on the Thursday of the same week. This time he was a little bored. After one more visit he determined never to enter her drawing-room again. Madame B—— went about declaring that Saint Clair was an ill-mannered young man of the worst style.

Saint Clair was born with a tender and affectionate heart, but, at an age when we too readily take impressions which we never get rid of, he had been laughed at by his friends for his effusive sentiments.

He was proud, he was ambitious, he was as sensitive as a child about what people thought of him. From that time he studiously tried to conceal what he regarded as a discreditable weakness. He succeeded, but the victory cost him dear. He could hide from the world the emotions of his heart, but the more he pent them up the more cruel they became. In society he had the unhappy reputation of caring for nothing and for nobody; when he was alone, his restless fancy caused him torments, none the less bitter because they were never suspected.

Verily it is hard to find a friend !

Difficult ! Is it even possible ? Have two men ever lived who had no secret from each other ?

Saint Clair did not believe in friendship, and his scepticism was known. People said that he was cold and reserved with men of his own age and set. He never asked them about their secrets, and most of his thoughts and actions were mysteries to them. The French love to talk about themselves, and thus

Saint Clair, in his own despite, was entrusted with many confidences. His friends—the men whom one meets twice a week I mean—complained of this lack of trustfulness, and indeed the man who volunteers his own secret is usually offended when we do not tell him ours. People think that indiscretion should be reciprocal.

"He is buttoned up to the chin," said Alphonse de Thémines, that handsome captain of horse, "I never could have the slightest confidence in that devil, Saint Clair."

"I believe he is a bit of a Jesuit," said Jules Lambert, "I have met him twice coming out of Saint Sulpice. Nobody knows what he has on his mind. I am never at my ease with him, for one."

The two friends parted company. Alphonse met Saint Clair on the Boulevard des Italiens, walking with his eyes on the ground and looking at nobody. He stopped Saint Clair, seized his arm, and had told him, before they reached the Rue de la Paix, all the story of his flirtation with Madame X——, whose husband was such a jealous brute.

The same evening, Jules Lambert lost his money at écarté, and, having no more to lose, took to dancing. In the waltz he jostled a man who had also lost his money, and who was in a bad humour. Sharp words followed, and a challenge. Jules Lambert instantly asked Saint Clair to be his second, and chose the opportunity to borrow money which he has consistently forgotten to pay back.

After all, Saint Clair was easy enough to live with. He was nobody's enemy but his own. He was good-natured, often good company, seldom tedious. He had travelled widely, had read widely, and his knowledge of books and of the world were never displayed when they had not been called for. For the rest, he was tall and handsome, there was no lack of nobility nor of genius in a face often too serious, but sweet and kindly when he smiled.

One point I was forgetting. To women Saint

Clair was always attentive, he preferred their conversation to that of his own sex. Was he in love? It was not easy to be certain, but, if that cold heart were touched at all, the beautiful Comtesse Mathilde de Coursy, a young widow at whose house he was a constant visitor, was known to be the favoured lady.

As to the closeness of their relations, there were the following grounds for an opinion: first, Saint Clair was ever most ceremoniously polite with the Comtesse, and she with him. Next, he seemed to make a point of never uttering her name, and certainly of never praising her in society. Third, before Saint Clair was presented to her, he was passionately fond of music and she of painting. Since their acquaintance began they had exchanged tastes. Finally, when the Comtesse went to take the waters last year, Saint Clair had followed her in a week.

*　　*　　*　　*　　*

The historian has his duties. Mine constrain me

to admit that, just before the sun rose from a night of July, the park gate of a country house opened, and a man slipped out as carefully as if he had been a burglar. Now this country house belonged to Madame de Coursy, and that man was Saint Clair. A woman, wrapped in a cloak, accompanied him to the gate, and peeped out to watch him departing by the path along the park wall. Saint Clair stopped, looked cautiously about, and waved his hand to bid the lady go back. In the clear summer night he could see her pale face, and see her standing motionless by the gate. He retraced his steps, drew near her, clasped her tenderly in his arms. He wished to make her promise to go in, but he had a hundred things to say to her. They may have talked together some ten minutes when they heard the voice of a peasant going forth to the labour of the fields. A kiss was given and taken, and instantly Saint Clair was at the end of the path.

He followed a road that seemed to be familiar to

him. Now he would leap for joy, would run like a child, cutting at the bushes with his cane; now again he would stop, or loiter slowly, watching the purple light flush up the sky from the dawning. Half an hour's walk brought him to the door of a little lonely house which he had rented for the season. He let himself in with his latch-key; he threw himself on a sofa, and with fixed eyes and a smiling mouth, he lost himself in day dreams. Nothing but happiness was in his thoughts. "How happy I am, how happy!" he kept saying to himself. "At length I have met a heart that can be at one with mine; my ideal is found at last. She is friend and mistress in one, and what a soul, what a heart of love! Love! no, she never loved another before me!"

Presently, his vanity glided in, as into all the things of this world it will glide.

"She is the most beautiful woman in Paris," he thought, and memory drew the picture of all her charms. "She has chosen *me* out of all the world!

Every one was at her feet! That Colonel of Hussars, brave, handsome, not more than conveniently conceited; that young writing fellow who sketches and acts so well; that Russian Lovelace with his Balkan campaign; Count de T—— with his wit, his manners, his sabre scar on the brow, and she sent them all about their business. Then *I!*"

Here the old burden of his thoughts came in again, " How happy, how happy I am !"

Then he rose, and opened the window, for he could scarcely breathe; then he walked up and down and again fell back on the sofa.

We cannot be always in the clouds. Saint Clair was tired; he yawned, stretched himself. It was broad daylight, and time to think of sleeping. When he wakened, he saw by his watch that he had barely an hour to dress in, and hurry to Paris, where he was to lunch with some young men of his acquaintance.

*   *   *   *   *

Another bottle of champagne was uncorked. The reader may guess how many had preceded it. Suffice it that the moment had come when every one wishes to speak all at once, and when strong heads begin to be anxious about weak ones.

"I wish," cried Alphonse de Thémines, who was for ever talking about England, "that we had the custom of toasting our mistresses here, in Paris. Then we should find out who Saint Clair sighs for." And he filled his own glass and his friends'.

Saint Clair, a little vexed, was about to answer, when Jules Lambert interrupted him.

"I like the custom, and I follow it." Then, lifting his glass, "To all the milliners in Paris," he cried, "except the old, the halt, and the blind."

"Hurrah!" cried the young friends of England.

Saint Clair rose, glass in hand.

"Gentlemen," said he, "my heart is not so capacious as Jules'; but it is more constant, and the more deserving, because I have been severed

so long from the lady of my thoughts. But I am
sure you will approve my choice, unless you are
my rivals. To Judith Pasta, gentlemen! May we
soon see her back again, the first actress of
Europe!"

Thémines wanted to criticise the toast; but he
was interrupted by applause.

Saint Clair, having parried this thrust, fancied
himself safe for the rest of the day.

The conversation was directed to the play, to
politics, to Lord Wellington, to English horses;
and thence, by an easy and obvious transition, to
women. A good horse first, a pretty mistress next;
those are the things desirable in a young man's
eyes.

Next began a discussion as to how those coveted
objects were to be procured. Saint Clair, after
modestly apologising for his want of experience
in such delicate negotiations, decided that to be
singular, to be unlike other people, was the shortest

way to the heart of woman. But is there any general law, any short cut to singularity? He fancied not.

"According to you, then," said Jules, "a man who limps, or a hunchback, is more likely to succeed than a lover built on the usual lines?"

"You push the notion rather far," said Saint Clair; "but if I must, I accept all the consequences of my theory. For example, if I were a hunchback, I would not blow my brains out, and I would want to please the fair. In the first place, then, I would plead my suit with two sorts of women—the really tender-hearted first, and next, ladies who affect originality, eccentricity. To the former I would paint the sorrows of my lot, the cruelty of Nature, in my case. I would try to make them pity me, and I would manage to persuade them that I was capable of a passionate affection. I would shoot one of my rivals in a duel, and then I would poison myself unsuccessfully with laudanum. In a few months my hump would have vanished in that lady's eyes, and then I would wait my chance. As for the women who affect originality, *their* conquest is easy. Merely persuade them that no hunchback yet was ever lucky in love, and they will rush to provide that rule with an exception."

"What a Don Juan!" cried Jules.

"Let us get our legs broken," said Colonel Beaujeu, "as we have not the luck to be born with humps."

"I agree with Saint Clair," said Hector Roquantin, who was under five feet in height. "Every day one hears of fair ladies falling in love with men whom you tall fellows would never think of as rivals."

"Hector, would you mind ringing for another bottle?" said Thémines.

The dwarf got up, and every one smiled as he thought of the fable of the fox who lost his tail.

" For my part," said Thémines, with a satisfied glance at the mirror, "the longer I live, the more clearly I see that a well-cut coat and a face which will pass are the singularities that win hearts most." And he flicked a crumb from his coat.

" Bah," said the little Roquantin, "a passable face and a coat of Stulz's win a heart—for a week. For love, for what *I* call love, you need——"

" Do you want a crucial instance?" said Thémines, interrupting. "You all knew Massigny? You all remember the kind of man he was? The manners of a groom; no more conversation than his horse. But he was as handsome as Adonis; he tied a tie like Brummell! And he was the greatest bore I ever knew."

" He nearly was the death of me," said the Colonel. "I once had to travel six hundred miles with him."

" He really *was* the death of poor Dick Thornton!" said Saint Clair.

"Why, Thornton was killed by brigands. Don't you know, at Fondi?" answered Jules.

"Yes, but Massigny was an accessory before the fact. Thornton and a lot of other men had agreed to travel to Naples together for fear of brigands. Massigny wanted to join the caravan. No sooner did Thornton hear of it than he set out alone, at once, and you know what came of it."

"Thornton was right: of two deaths he chose the gentler," said Thémines. "Any fellow would have done the same. . . . Well," he said, after a pause, "you admit Massigny was the greatest bore on earth."

"Right," cried everybody.

"Let us cause no man to despair," said Jules. "Let us make an exception in favour of X——, especially when he gets on politics."

"You will next grant," said Thémines, "that Madame de Coursy is a woman of wit, if ever there was one?"

There was a moment's silence. Saint Clair took an immense interest in the flowers painted on his plate.

"*I* maintain," said Jules, raising his voice, "that she is one of the three pleasantest women in Paris."

"I knew her husband," said the Colonel. "He often showed me delightful letters of hers."

"Auguste," said little Roquantin, "introduce me to the Comtesse. They say you can do anything with her."

"Next winter, perhaps," muttered Saint Clair, "when she comes back to Paris: I—I believe she sees nobody in the country."

"Will you listen to me?" cried Thémines.

Silence was restored. Saint Clair fidgeted on his seat like a prisoner at the bar.

"You did not know the Comtesse three years ago, Saint Clair. You were in Germany then," said Thémines, taking up his tale with provoking deliberation. "You can't imagine how pretty she was then—fresh as a rose, full of life, gay as a butterfly. Well, of all her admirers, who do you suppose was the fortunate man?—Massigny! The dullest man and the most dreary turned the heart of the wittiest of women. Do you think a hunchback would have had the luck? Nonsense! Good looks, a good tailor, enterprise,—these suffice."

Saint Clair's position was cruel. To give Thémines the lie direct was to compromise the Comtesse. He might have said something on her side; but his tongue clave to the roof of his mouth. His lips trembled with rage, and he vainly cast about for some other pretext of quarrel.

"What!" cried Jules with an air of surprise; "Madame de Coursy was Massigny's mistress? 'Frailty, thy name is woman'!"

"A woman's reputation," said Saint Clair, contemptuously; "what is it? Any one may play the wit with it; any one may tear it to tatters."

As he spoke, he remembered with horror a

certain Etruscan vase that he had seen hundreds of times on the chimneypiece of the Comtesse in Paris. He knew that it had been a present from Massigny, on his return from Italy, and—an aggravating circumstance—this vase had been brought from Paris to the country. Moreover, every evening Mathilde put her bouquet in this very vase!

The words died on his lips; he could see nothing, he could think of nothing, but the Etruscan vase.

"Admirable proof!" cries the critic; "and a gallant sort of testimony to suspect a mistress on!"

Were *you* ever in love, dear critic?

Thémines was in too good humour to be offended by the tone of Saint Clair. He answered with gay good nature:

"I only repeat what every one says. When you were in Germany, the case seemed a certainty. However, I scarcely know Madame de Coursy. I have not seen her for a year and a half. Everybody may have been wrong. Massigny may have fabled;

but, to return to the subject, even if the example is false, it does not follow that I am not right. You know the cleverest woman in France, whose works——"

The door opened, and Theodore Neville entered: home from Egypt.

"Theodore!"   "Back already?"   A shower of questions fell about him.

"Have you brought a Turkish costume?" asked Thémines.   "Have you an Arab horse, and an Egyptian groom?"

"What is the Pasha like?   When is he going to assert his independence?   Have you seen a head fall at one sabre stroke?"

"And the *Almées?*" cried Roquantin.   "Are the Cairo women pretty?"

"And the pyramids?"

"And the cataracts?"

"And the statue of Memnon?"

"And Ibrahim Pacha?"

Everybody spoke at once. Saint Clair was brooding on the Etruscan vase.

Theodore sat down crossed-legged, Egyptian fashion; waited till the questioners were weary, and then spoke quickly, not to be interrupted.

"The pyramids! Regular humbug! Not so high as they say. The cathedral at Strasburg is within twelve feet of it. I'm sick of antiquities; don't speak of them. Show me a hieroglyph and I faint. So many tourists worry over hieroglyphs. For my part, I wanted to study the odd crowd that fills the streets of Alexandria and Cairo: Turks, Bedouins, Copts, Fellahs, Arabs."

"How long were you in Egypt then?"

"Six weeks."

And he went on describing everything, from the cedar of Lebanon to the hyssop on the wall.

Saint Clair left the room almost as soon as the traveller entered it, and rode home, galloping too hard to think consecutively. But he had a vague sense that his happiness in this world was lost for ever, and nobody to blame but a dead man and a vase of dead Etruria.

Once at home, he threw himself on the very sofa where, in the morning, he had made that long delicious analysis of his own happiness. The idea which had given him the most exquisite delight was this, that *his* mistress was *not* "a very, very woman." Nay, she had never loved, could never love another, but him only. And now this goodly dream was taking flight before the cold reality.

"I have a pretty mistress, and there's an end of it. Witty she is, and all the more blame to her for having loved Massigny. True, she loves me now with all the soul she has. To be loved as Massigny was loved—what a triumph! She has yielded to my importunity, my attentions. Nobody has deceived me but myself. There was no sympathy between our hearts; Massigny or myself, it was all one to her. He was handsome; she loved him for that. I am lucky enough to amuse her, so 'Let me love Saint Clair,' says she, 'as the other is dead. And if Saint Clair dies, or begins to bore me, then we shall see.'"

I firmly believe that the devil is present, invisible, listening, listening while unhappy men torment themselves thus. It is good sport for Satan, and when the victim's wounds are beginning to close, there is the devil present to open them again.

So it was with Saint Clair. He seemed to hear a voice that murmured in his ear,—

> "*l'honneur singulier*
> *D'être successeur* . . . "

Up he leaped, and cast a wild glance round him. Glad would he have been to find some one in his room, and to slay him with his hands.

The clock struck eight. At half-past eight the Comtesse expected him. Should he break tryst?

"Why *should* I go back and see Massigny's mistress?" he asked himself.

He lay down on the sofa, and shut his eyes. "Let me sleep," he said, remaining motionless for exactly half a minute. Then he leaped up, and ran to the clock to see how the time went. "How I wish it were half-past eight," he thought; "then it would be too late to start." He had not the courage to stay at home, without an excuse. He would have liked to be ill. He walked the room, he sat down, he took a book, he could not read one syllable. He sat down before the piano, without the energy to open it. He whistled, stared at the clouds, thought of trying to count the poplars in front of his window. At last he looked at the clock again. He had succeeded in killing just three minutes.

"I can't help loving her," he said, grinding his teeth, and stamping his foot; "she is my tyrant, I am her slave, as Massigny was before me. Well, wretch, obey, as you have not the courage to break the chain you hate."

He took his hat and rushed out, slowly climbing the path which led to the park gate. Far off he saw a white figure standing out against the darkness of the trees. She waved a handkerchief; his heart beat violently, his knees trembled, he could not have spoken; and was so nervous that he was afraid the Comtesse might see his ill humour in his face.

She held out her hand, so he kissed it; she threw herself on his breast, so he kissed her brow; she led him on, and he followed, followed her to her chamber, silent, struggling with the sighs that seemed as if they would burst his breast.

A single candle gave all the light in the boudoir of the Comtesse. The twain sat down, and Saint Clair's eye fell on his lady's locks, and the one rose iu her hair.

The night before he had brought her an English engraving, the Duchess of Portland, after Lely, in which her Grace's hair is dressed in this way. "I like that rose better than all your miracles of hairdressing," Saint Clair had said, for he disliked jewels, and agreed with the English peer's remark—"The devil himself is no judge of a horse in harness, or of a woman in her war-paint."

The night before Saint Clair had said, as he played with a pearl necklace (he liked to have something in his hands when he spoke), "Jewels are of no use but to hide blemishes. You are too beautiful to need them, Mathilde." So this evening, the Comtesse, who noted his lightest word, wore neither bracelets, rings, earrings, nor necklace. Saint Clair looked at a woman's *chaussure* before any other part of her dress. Like many men, he had extreme ideas on this matter. Now, as it chanced, a heavy shower had fallen before sunset. The grass was still wet, but the Comtesse was walking on the damp turf in silk stockings and satin shoes.

"She loves me," thought St. Clair, and he sighed for himself over his own folly. Nor could he choose but smile when he looked at Mathilde, divided between his black moods, and the pleasure of seeing a beautiful woman striving to please him by all the nothings that lovers love.

As for the Comtesse, **her** face was bright with mingled love and mischief. She took some object from a box of Japanese lacquer, and held out her little hand, clenched, saying :

"I broke your watch some nights ago. Here it is, mended."

She handed him the watch, biting her lips to restrain her mirth. Ah, how white her teeth looked on those lips of rose !

A man makes a poor figure when he is cold to the playfulness of a pretty woman.

Saint Clair thanked her, took the watch, and put it in his pocket.

"Nay, look at it, open it," said she, "and see whether it has been well mended. You should know —you, that are so learned, a pupil of the École Polytechnique."

"Oh, I'm no judge of the matter," said Saint Clair. He opened the case with an absent air. Lo, there was a miniature of Madame de Coursy painted on the interior of the case! Who could sulk any longer? His face brightened; he forgot Massigny, he only remembered that he was with a charming woman, and she loved him.

*   *   *   *   *

The lark, that herald of the dawn, began to sing, and long, pale lines of light furrowed the eastern clouds. 'Tis the hour when Romeo bids farewell to Juliet, the classic hour of lovers' partings.

Saint Clair was standing by a chimney-piece, the key of the park gate in his hand, gazing at the Etruscan vase, to which, at the bottom of his heart, he still bore a grudge. However, he was in good humour, and the simple idea that Thémines might have lied was beginning to occur to him. While the Comtesse, who was to accompany him to the gate, wrapped her head in a shawl, he gently struck the detestable vase with the key, gradually increasing the strength of each tap, so that it seemed as if he would presently make it fly into a dozen fragments.

"Ah, take care!" cried Mathilde, "you will break my beautiful Etruscan vase," and she snatched the key from his hands.

Saint Clair was much displeased, but he submitted. He turned his back to the chimney-piece to avoid temptation, and began to examine the portrait which had just been given to him.

"Who painted it?" he asked.

"Monsieur R——. It was Massigny who told me of him." (Massigny, since his tour to Rome, had developed an exquisite taste in art, and was the patron of all the young painters.) "I believe it is like, though it is a little flattered."

Saint Clair was tempted to dash the watch against the wall; but he mastered himself, and replaced it in his pocket. Then, becoming aware that it was already day, he left the house, begging Mathilde to let him go alone, crossed the park with long strides, and was presently in the open country.

"Massigny, Massigny everywhere!" he cried. "Of course, the painter who did this made another for Massigny. Idiot that I was for believing that I was loved with a love like my own, merely because she wore no jewels and a rose in her hair! Jewels! she has a chest full of them; Massigny cared for nothing else. Ah, she has a charmingly accommodating humour, and readily falls in with the tastes of her lovers. I would rather a hundred times that she were a courtesan, selling herself for money!"

Presently another, and not less unhappy, idea occurred to him. In a few weeks the Comtesse would be out of mourning. Now Saint Clair was to marry her as soon as her first year of widowhood was over. He had promised this, or not exactly promised, for he had never spoken of it; but this had been his intention, and so the Comtesse had understood it. To Saint Clair this understanding was no less sacred than an oath. A night ago, and he would have given a throne to hasten the moment when he might publicly avow his love. But now he shuddered at the bare idea of uniting his lot with that of the mistress of Massigny.

"And yet it is my duty, and I will," he muttered. "No doubt she thought I knew the story of her old intrigue; it seems to have been public enough. Besides, she did not, she cannot understand me. She thinks my love is like Massigny's!"

Then he thought, and not without pride, "For three months she made me the happiest of men, and *that* deserves the sacrifice of the rest of my life."

He did not go home, but rode through the forests all the morning. In the wood of Verrières he saw a man far off, mounted on an English thoroughbred, and the man hailed him by name. It was Alphonse de Thémines. To any one in Saint Clair's mood loneliness is as welcome as the meeting with Thémines was the reverse, St. Clair's

ill humour became a stifled passion of anger. Thémines never noticed it, or took a malicious pleasure
in irritating Saint Clair.

He chatted, laughed, jested, without observing
that he was unanswered. Saint Clair turned his
horse down a narrow ride, hoping that the bore
would not follow him; but a bore does not so lightly
release his prey. Thémines turned and made better
speed to ride abreast with Saint Clair, and so con-
verse more easily.

The ride, as I said, was narrow. Two horses could
scarcely move abreast in it, so it is not surprising
that Thémines, though an excellent horseman, brushed
roughly against Saint Clair's foot, as he came level
with him.

Saint Clair could control himself no longer; he
rose in his stirrups, and brought his whip down with
all his might on the nose of Thémines' horse.

" What the devil is the matter with you, Auguste?"
cried Thémines; " why do you strike my horse ?"

"Why do you follow me?" answered Saint Clair in a terrible voice.

"Are you mad, Saint Clair? Do you forget that you are speaking to *me?*"

"I know that I am speaking to a conceited fool."

"I believe you are out of your mind, Saint Clair. Listen, to-morrow you will apologise, or you must give me satisfaction."

"To-morrow be it, sir."

Thémines reined in his horse, Saint Clair spurred his on; presently he disappeared in the wood.

He felt calmer now, for he believed in presentiments, he had a presentiment that he would fall to-morrow, and there would be an end. One more day to live, and to-morrow,—his torments, his doubts would be over. He went home, sent his man with a note to Colonel Beaujeu, wrote some letters, dined with a good appetite, and, at half-past eight was punctual at the gates of the park.

"What is the matter with you to-day, Auguste?"

said the Comtesse. "You are in strange high spirits, and yet you don't make me laugh; yesterday you were rather dismal, and I was merry; to-day we have changed characters. For my part, I have a headache."

"Yes, dear," he said, "I own I was dull yesterday. But to-day, I have been riding, taking exercise; I never was better."

"I rose late, I slept long this morning, I had horrible dreams."

"Dreams! Do you believe in dreams?"

"Nonsense, of course not!"

"I believe in them, and I wager you have had one that bodes calamity."

"Really, I never remember my dreams. Yet I seem to remember,—in my dream I saw Massigny, so you see it could not have been very diverting!"

"Massigny! I fancied you would have been delighted to see him again!"

"Poor Massigny!"

"Poor Massigny?"

"Auguste, I implore you tell me what is the matter with you to-night. There is something diabolical in your smile. You look as you do when you are with people you dislike."

"Ah, now you are treating me as ill as your friends the old dowagers; give me your hand!"

He kissed her hand with a mocking gallantry. For a minute they gazed at each other.

Saint Clair was the first to look down. "How hard it is," he cried, "to live in this world, without passing for ill-natured! One should never speak of anything but the weather, or sport, or talk over the finance of their philanthropies with some of your old friends."

He took a paper from a table.

"Look, here is your washerwoman's bill. Let us talk about *that*, my angel, and you will not be able to call me cruel."

"Auguste, you amaze me."

"Your washerwoman's handwriting makes me think of a letter which I found this morning, when I was arranging my papers, a love-letter from a dress-maker whom I adored at sixteen. She has her own way of writing every word, and that way is always the most complicated. Her style is worthy of her spelling. Well, as I was more or less conceited then, I felt that I could not tolerate a mistress who was not a Sévigne. I broke with her suddenly. To-day, as I read her letter again, I saw that this milliner had really loved me."

"What, a woman whom you kept?"

"In splendour! on fifty francs a month. My guardian did not make me a large allowance."

"And what became of the girl?"

"How should I know? dead in a hospital, probably."

"Auguste, if it were so, you would not put on that air of nonchalance."

"Well, to tell the strict truth, she married a decent

sort of fellow, and when I came of age I gave her a little dowry."

"How good you are! and why do you prefer to seem bad?"

"Oh, I am very, very good. The more I think of it, the more I am sure that she really loved me. But at that time I could not detect a real sentiment under an absurd disguise."

"You should have brought me the letter. I should not have been jealous. We women have more tact than you, and the mere style of a note will tell us whether the writer is serious or not."

"And yet how many times you let yourselves be wheedled by fools or fops," and as he spoke he looked at the Etruscan vase with a sinister expression which escaped Mathilde.

"Oh, you men, you all wish to pass for Don Juans! You think you are deceiving women, when just as often as not you meet *Donna Juanas*, as bad as yourselves."

"I fancied, madam, that with your wit, you detected a dullard a mile off. Then I doubt not that our friend Massigny, who was a stupid fop, died a virgin martyr."

"But Massigny was not so very stupid; and besides, there are the stupid women. I must tell you a story about Massigny. But have I never told it to you before?"

"Never!" said Saint Clair. His voice trembled as he spoke.

"Well, Massigny fell in love with me when he came back from Italy. My husband knew him, and introduced him to me as a man of taste, a wit! They were born to appreciate each other. Massigny gave me sketches he said were his own, he uttered art criticisms in the most diverting way; finally he sent me a letter in which he said that I was the best woman in Paris, and that therefore he wished me to be his mistress. This letter I showed to my cousin Julie, and as we were both wild girls, we determined to play him a trick. Julie said to me one evening, when Massigny was with us, 'I shall read you a declaration that I got this morning,' and she actually read it among peals of laughter. Poor Massigny!"

Saint Clair fell on his knees with a cry of joy. He seized the Comtesse's hand, he covered it with tears and kisses.

"I am the worst of men, and the maddest," he said; "for two days I have been suspecting you, and I have not asked you for an explanation."

"You suspected me,—of what?"

"Oh, I am a wretch,—of having loved Massigny!"

"Massigny!"

She began to laugh, and then more seriously: "Auguste, were you really mad enough to suspect such a thing, and unfair enough to hide your suspicions?"

Tears came into her eyes as she spoke.

"Forgive me, I implore you."

"Of course, I shall forgive you, but first hear me swear."

"Oh, I believe you, I believe you."

"But, in heaven's name, what could make you imagine such a thing?"

"Nothing, but my own folly, and that confounded vase, which I knew Massigny gave you."

The Comtesse clasped her hands in amazement; then she broke out into peals of laughter. "My Etruscan vase! My Etruscan vase!"

Saint Clair could not but laugh himself, though there were tears on his cheeks. He caught Mathilde in his arms, crying, "I shall never let you go till you pardon me."

"Yes, I forgive you, *mon ami*," she said, kissing him tenderly. "You make me very happy; it is the first time I have seen you weep; I thought you had no tears."

Then, slipping from his arms, she seized the vase and dashed it into a thousand pieces on the floor.

It was a rare unpublished piece, with a combat of a Centaur, and one of the Lapithæ in three colours.

For some hours Saint Clair was the happiest and humblest of men.

*   *   *   *   *

"Well," said Roquantin to Colonel Beaujeu, whom he met at Tortoni's in the evening, "the news is true!"

"Too true," said the Colonel sadly.

"How did it all happen?"

"All as it should. Saint Clair began by telling me that he was in the wrong, but that he wished to stand Thémines' fire before apologising. Of course I had to agree. Thémines wanted to draw lots for first fire Saint Clair insisted that he should fire first. Thémines fired. I saw St. Clair turn round once, and he fell stone dead. I have often noticed that odd wheeling round in soldiers hit in battle."

"It is strange," said Roquantin. "And what did Thémines do?"

" Oh, just what he should have done ! Threw down his pistol and looked sorry. Indeed, he threw it so hard that he broke the hammer, and as it was a Manton, I doubt if there is a gunmaker in Paris who can make him another."

For three years the Comtesse lived alone, and saw nobody, except a mulatto woman, who was in the secret of her *liaison*. At the end of three years her cousin Julie, returned from a long tour, insisted on seeing Mathilde, and found her the ghost of herself. She induced the Comtesse to winter at Hyères, where she languished for a few months, and died of consumption, brought on by regret, according to Dr. M——, who attended her.

THE DOCTOR'S STORY.

(HONORÉ DE BALZAC.)

ABOUT a hundred yards from the town of Vendôme,
on the borders of the Loir, there is an old grey
house, surmounted by very high gables, and so completely isolated that neither tanyard, nor shabby
hostelry, such as you may find at the entrance to
all small towns, exist in its immediate neighbourhood.

In front of this building, overlooking the river, is
a garden, where the once well-trimmed box borders,
that used to define the walks, now grow wild as they
list. Several willows that spring from the Loir have
grown as rapidly as the hedge that encloses it, and
half conceal the house. The rich vegetation of

those weeds that we call foul adorns the sloping shore. Fruit trees, neglected for the last ten years, no longer yield their harvest, and their shoots form coppices. The wall-fruit grows like hedges against the walls. Paths once gravelled are overgrown with moss, but, to tell the truth, there is no trace of a path. From the height of the hill, to which cling the ruins of the old castle of the Dukes of Vendôme, the only spot whence the eye can plunge into this enclosure, it strikes you that, at a time not easy to determine, this plot of land was the delight of a country gentleman, who cultivated roses and tulips and horticulture in general, and who was besides a lover of fine fruit. An arbour is still visible, or rather the *débris* of an arbour, where there is a table that time has not quite destroyed. The aspect of this garden of bygone days suggests the negative joys of peaceful provincial life, as one might reconstruct the life of a worthy tradesman by reading the epitaph on his tombstone. As if to complete the sweetness and the sadness of the ideas that possess one's soul, one of the walls displays a sun-dial decorated with the following commonplace Christian inscription: "ULTIMAM COGITA!" The roof of this house is horribly dilapidated, the shutters are always closed, the balconies are covered with swallows' nests, the doors are perpetually shut, weeds have drawn green lines in the cracks of the flights of steps, the locks and bolts are rusty. Sun, moon, winter, summer and snow have worn the panelling, warped the boards, gnawed the paint. The lugubrious silence which reigns there is only broken by birds, cats, martins, rats and mice, free to course to and fro, to fight and to eat each other. Everywhere an invisible hand has graven the word *mystery*.

Should your curiosity lead you to glance at this house from the side that points to the road, you would perceive a great door which the children of the place have riddled with holes. I afterwards heard that this door had been closed for the last ten years.

Through the holes broken by the boys you would have observed the perfect harmony that existed between the façades of both garden and courtyard. In both the same disorder prevails. Tufts of weeds encircle the paving stones. Enormous cracks furrow the walls, round whose blackened crests twine the thousand garlands of the pellitory. The steps are out of joint, the wire of the bell is rusted, the spouts are cracked. What fire from heaven has fallen here? What tribunal has decreed that salt should be strewn on this dwelling? Has God been blasphemed, has France been here betrayed? These are the questions we ask ourselves, but get no answer from the crawling things that haunt the place. This empty and deserted house is a gigantic enigma, of which the key is lost. In bygone times it was a small fief, and bears the name of the *Grande Bretêche*.

During the time of my sojourn in Vendôme, where Despleins had left me in charge of a wealthy patient, the sight of this singular dwelling became one of my greatest pleasures. Was it not better than a ruin? To a ruin belong certain memories of an irrefutable authenticity. But this habitation which was no ruin, albeit in slow process of demolition by a vengeful hand, hid a secret, an unknown idea; to say the least, it spoke of unaccountable caprice. More than once in the evening I paused at the overgrown hedge that protected this enclosure. In defiance of scratches, I entered the garden without a master, the property which was no longer either public or private, and I spent hours in the contemplation of its disorder. Not even for the sake of its history, to which doubtless this singular spectacle was due, would I have consented to address a single question to a loquacious native of Vendôme. There I wove delightful romances, I gave myself up to little feasts of an enchanting melancholy. If I had learned the possibly commonplace motive of this neglect, I might have lost all the unpublished poesy that so intoxicated my fancy.

This secluded spot represented to my mind the most varied aspects of human life, o'ershadowed by its misfortunes. At times it had the air of a cloister without monks, at others it was the peace of the graveyard, undisturbed by the mortuary eloquence of the tombstone and the dead; to-day it was the leper's dwelling, to-morrow it was the House of the Atridæ. But above all it represented provincial life in its withdrawn meditation, its hourglass existence. I have often wept, I have never smiled there. Many a time as the fleet wings of a wild dove passed over me with their dull, soft, whizzing sound, I have been seized with an involuntary horror of fear. The soil is damp; you need to beware of lizards, vipers and frogs, that disport themselves therein in the wild freedom of nature. Above all, you must not mind the cold, for in a few moments you will feel an icy mantle descend upon your shoulders, like the hand of the commander on the throat of Don Juan. One evening I shuddered; the wind had turned a rusty weather cock, whose cries were like a groan breathed by the house itself, at the very moment that I terminated a somewhat sombre drama, by the aid of which I explained to myself the singular and enduring melancholy of the scene. I returned to my inn, a prey to gloomy thoughts. When I had supped, the landlady entered my room with an air of mystery and said to me,—

"Sir, here is Monsieur Regnault."

"Who is Monsieur Regnault?"

"Why, Monsieur does not know Monsieur Regnault? Ah! that is curious," she said, as she walked away.

Suddenly I saw a long, spare man appear, clothed in black and holding his hat in his hand, who presented himself like a ram about to rush at his rival, while to me he exhibited a retreating forehead, a little, pointed head, and a livid face, not unlike a glass of dirty water. You would have taken him for an usher in a Government office. The unknown wore an old coat, very worn at the seams; but there was a diamond in the *jabot* of his shirt, and he had gold rings in his ears.

"Sir," I said, "with whom have I the honour of speaking?"

He seated himself on a chair, placed his hat on my table, and replied, rubbing his hands,—

"Ah! it's very cold. Sir, I am Monsieur Regnault."

I bowed, and said to myself,—

"*Il bondo cani.* Find it——"

"I am," he added, "a notary of Vendôme."

"Sir, I am charmed!" I cried; "but for reasons known to myself, I am not disposed to make my will."

"One moment!" he answered, raising his hand as if to enjoin silence. "Permit me, sir, permit me. I have heard that you sometimes walk in the garden of the *Grande Bretéche.*"

"Yes, sir."

"One moment!" he said, reiterating his gesture. "This act is a regular misdemeanour. Sir, I come in the name and as the testamentary executor of the late Comtesse de Merret to beg you to discontinue your visits. One moment! I am not a Turk, and I don't want to make a crime of it. Besides, you are quite welcome to ignore the circumstances that oblige me to let the finest *hotel* of Vendôme fall into decay. Yet, sir, you appear to be an educated person, and should therefore be aware that the law prohibits, under penalty of condign punishment, the invasion of enclosed property. A hedge is as good as a wall. But the actual state of the house may serve as an excuse for your curiosity. I could wish for nothing better than to let you go and come in the house; but as it is my office to see that the will of the testatrix be respected, I have the honour, sir, to request you not to enter the garden again. I myself, sir, since the reading of the will,—I have not set foot in that house which belongs, as I have had the honour of informing you, to the estate. of Madame de Merret. All we did was to ascertain the number of the doors and windows, so as to fix the taxes, which I pay annually out of funds set aside for this purpose by Madame la Comtesse. Ah! my dear sir, her will made a sensation in Vendôme!"

Here he stopped to blow his nose—the worthy man! I respected his loquaciousness, understanding as well as possible that the inheritance of Madame de Merret was the most important event in his life,—his reputation, his glory, his Restoration. I had to say farewell to my fine reveries and romances; I was therefore no longer averse to learning the truth from an official source.

"Sir," I said, "would it be indiscreet to ask you the cause of this eccentricity?"

At these words, an air that expressed all the pleasure of mounting his hobby-horse passed over the face of the notary. He turned up his shirt collar with a sort of foppishness, drew out his snuff-box, opened it, offered me snuff; and on my refusal seized a huge pinch. He was happy. A man who keeps no hobby does not know how much can be got out of life. A hobby is the middle course between a passion and a monomania. At that moment, I fully realized the delightful expression of Sterne, and I had a perfect idea of the joy with which Uncle Toby, aided by Trim, mounted his war-horse.

"Sir," said Monsieur Regnault, "I have been head clerk to Maître Rogain in Paris. Excellent house, doubtless known to you by name? No! Yet it was celebrated through an unfortunate failure. I had not sufficient capital for Paris, at the price practices were worth in 1816. I came here and bought the practice of my predecessor. I had some relations in Vendôme,—among others a very rich aunt, who gave me her daughter to wife. Sir," he continued after a short pause, "three months after I had been licensed by the Lord Keeper of the Seals, I was summoned, just as I was going to bed (I was not yet married) by the Comtesse de Merret, to her *château* of Merret. Her maid, a good creature who now serves in this inn, was waiting at my door with the carriage of Madame la Comtesse.

"Ah! one moment! I must tell you, sir, that the Comte de Merret had gone to Paris to die, two months before I arrived here. He there died a miserable death, having given himself up to every species of excess. You understand? The day he went the Countess had left the *Grande Bretéche* and had stripped it of its furniture. There are those who aver that she burnt the furniture, the tapestry, in fact all those articles whatsoever, of and pertaining to the habitation at present let to the aforesaid. . . . (Well, what am I talking about? I beg your pardon; I fancied I was dictating a lease.) That she burnt them," he continued, "in the meadow at

Merret. Have you been to Merret, sir? No," he said, replying to himself for me. "Ah! it is a fine spot. For about three months," he continued, after a little shake of the head, "the Count and the Countess had led a singular life. They received nobody; Madame lived on the ground floor, Monsieur on the first. When the Countess was left alone, she went nowhere but to church. Later, at her *château,* she refused to see the friends who came to visit her. She was already very changed at the time she left the *Grande Bretêche* for Merret. That dear woman. . . . (I say dear, because this diamond comes to me from her, yet I have never seen her but once.) Well, the good lady was very ill; she had doubtless given herself up, for she died without consenting to call in any doctors; and indeed many of our ladies have thought that she was not quite in her right mind. Sir, my curiosity was uncommonly roused when I heard that Madame de Merret needed my services.

I was not the only person who was interested in that story. That very evening, although it was late, the whole town knew that I was going to Merret. The maid replied very vaguely to the questions I put to her on the way; still she told me that the *Curé* of Merret had administered the Sacrament to her mistress in the course of the day, and that she was unlikely to live through the night. I arrived at the *château* at about eleven o'clock, and went up the grand staircase. After passing through several high, dark rooms—devilishly cold and damp,—I reached the state bedroom, where Madame la Comtesse was. From the report that has been spread about the lady, (sir, I should never end, were I to repeat to you all the stories that were current about her,) I imagined her to be a coquette. Would you believe that I had some difficulty in making her out in the great bed where she lay? Indeed, the only light in this enormous chamber, hung with old-world tapestries, dusty enough to make you sneeze if you only looked at them, was one of those antique argand lamps. Ah! but you have not been to Merret. Well, sir, the bed is one of those beds of other days, with a high tester, upholstered with flowered chintz. A little table stood near the bed, and on it I perceived an *Imitation de Jésus Christ*, which, by the way, I bought for my wife, as well as the lamps. There were also a large arm-chair, for the housekeeper, and two chairs. No fire, however. That was the furniture. It would not have made ten lines in an inventory.

"Ah! my dear sir, had you seen, as I then saw, that vast chamber hung with sombre tapestry, you would have fancied yourself transported into a chapter of a romance. It was icy, and more than that, funereal," he added, raising his hand with a theatrical gesture and pausing. "By dint of straining my sight, and after approaching the bed, I at last discovered Madame de Merret, and then only thanks to the light of the lamp that fell upon the pillows. Her face was as yellow as wax, and so sharp that it looked like two clasped hands. Madame la Comtesse wore a lace cap, which allowed her beautiful hair, that was now snow-white, to escape. She was in a sitting posture, that she appeared to maintain with much difficulty. Her great dark eyes, that were doubtless spent by fever and scarcely living, hardly moved under the arch of her eyebrows—these," he said, showing me the orbit of his eyes. "Her brow was moist. Her emaciated hands were like bones, covered with soft skin; her veins, her muscles were perfectly visible. She must have been most beautiful; but I cannot tell you the impression her aspect made upon me at that moment. According to those who buried her, no mortal ever lived who was so wasted. In fact it was a frightful sight! Disease had so worn the woman that she was no more than a shadow. Her pale violet lips appeared motionless to me when she spoke. Although my profession had familiarized me with sights such as these, being frequently called to the bedsides of the dying to attest their last wills, I confess that the weeping families and the death struggles that I have witnessed were nothing in comparison to that silent and solitary woman, in that vast *château*. I heard not the slightest sound, I did not perceive the movement that the invalid's breathing should have communicated to the clothes that covered her, and I stood motionless, absorbed in a contemplation that was like a stupor. I can fancy I am there now. At last her great eyes moved, she attempted to raise her right hand, it fell back upon the bed, and these words escaped her lips like a breath, for her voice was no longer a voice: 'I have been expecting you anxiously.' Her cheeks flushed violently. Speaking, sir, was an effort to her. 'Madame,' I said to her. She signed to me to be silent. Then the old housekeeper rose and whispered in my ear: 'Do not speak; Madame la Comtesse is in no state to bear the slightest noise; anything you said to her might agitate her.' I sat down. A few moments later, Madame de Merret availed herself of all her remaining strength to move her right arm, and placed it, not without infinite trouble, under her coverlid. She waited a moment; then, with a last effort, she withdrew her hand with a sealed paper. Drops of sweat fell from her brow. 'I give into your charge my last will and testament. Ah! my God! Ah!' That was all. She grasped a crucifix that lay upon the bed, carried it rapidly to her lips, and died. I still shiver to think of the expression of her fixed eyes. She must have suffered so much! There was joy in her dying gaze, a joy that remained imprinted in her dead eyes. I took the will away, and when it was opened, I found that Madame de Merret had named me her testamentary executor. She left the whole of her personalty to the hospital of Vendôme, minus certain private legacies. But her

disposal of the *Grande Bretêche* is as follows:—
She desired me to leave this house for the term of
fifty years, counting from the day of her death,
exactly as it would be found at the time of her
demise, refusing admittance to the apartments to
any person whatsoever, and with a prohibition as
to the smallest repairs. At the same time she
allowed an income, if necessary, to pay guardians
who would insure the carrying out of her intentions.
On the expiration of this term, if the wishes of the
testatrix have been respected, the house is to belong
to my heirs, for you are aware, sir, that a notary
may not accept a legacy. Otherwise the *Grande
Bretêche* will pass to the heir-at-law, on condition of
his fulfilling the clauses indicated in a codicil annexed
to the will, which codicil is not to be read before
the expiration of the said fifty years. The will
has not been contested, therefore . . ." At these
words, without finishing his sentence, the oblong
notary regarded me with an air of triumph.

I made him quite happy by the compliments I then paid him.

"Sir," I said in conclusion, "you have produced so vivid an impression on me, that I fancy I can see the dying woman, paler than her sheets; her shining eyes frighten me, I shall dream of her to-night. But you must have formed some opinion as to the conditions of this eccentric will."

"Sir," he replied with a kind of comic reserve, "I never venture to judge the conduct of persons who honour me by the gift of a diamond."

I soon unlocked the tongue of the scrupulous notary of Vendôme, who communicated to me, not without long digressions, observations due to the astute policy of the two sexes * who frame the laws of Vendôme. But so diffuse and con- tradictory were these observations, that, despite my interest in this authentic history, I nearly

---

* Women and priests.

went to sleep. The heavy tones and monotonous accent of the notary, doubtless accustomed to listen to himself and to be listened to by his fellow citizens, got the better of my curiosity. Fortunately, he took his departure.

"Ah! ah! sir," he said on the staircase, "many people would like to live another five-and-forty years; but, one moment!" And with an air of wisdom, he placed his right hand against his nostrils, as if to say: "Now pay particular attention to this!" "To get so far," he said, "one must needs be under sixty."

I closed my door, after being awakened from my apathy by this last shaft which the notary considered very witty; then I seated myself in my arm-chair, placing my feet on the two fire-dogs of my hearth. I lost myself in a romance *à la* Radcliffe, based on the legal data of Monsieur Regnault, when my door, impelled by the cunning hand of woman, turned on its hinges. I saw my hostess approach, a fat, good-tempered body, who had missed her vocation, that of a Fleming in a picture by Teniers.

"Well, sir," she said, "Monsieur Regnault has doubtless treated you to his tale of the *Grande Bretêche ?* "

"Yes, Dame Lepas."

"What has he told you ? "

I repeated to her in a few words the chill and gloomy history of Madame de Merret. After every sentence my landlady craned her neck, regarding me the while with the perspicacity of an innkeeper, a sort of medium between the instincts of a policeman, the guile of a spy, and the cunning of a tradesman.

"My dear Dame Lepas ! " I added in conclusion, "you appear to know more about it, *hein ?* If not, what have you come here about ? "

"Ah ! on my honour as an honest woman, as true as my name is Lepas——"

"Don't swear; your eyes are big with mystery. You knew Monsieur de Merret; what sort of a man was he?"

"*Dame*, you see, Monsieur de Merret was a fine man you could never see enough of, he was so long! a worthy gentleman who came from Picardy, and *whose cap was a tight fit for his head*, as we say here. He paid ready money to avoid disputes with any one. You see, he was so peppery! Our ladies all admired him."

"Because he was peppery?" said I to my landlady.

"Perhaps," she said. "You see, sir, that there must have been something in him, so to speak, for him to have married the greatest beauty and heiress of the country. She had about twenty thousand francs a year. All the town was at the wedding. The bride was lovely and gracious, a gem of a little woman. Ah! they were a handsome couple in their day!"

" Were they happy in their married life ?"

" So, so, yes and no, as far as we could tell, for you can imagine that we did not live on terms of equality with them ! Madame de Merret was a good creature, so nice, who perhaps had a great deal to put up with through her husband's temper; but although he was rather proud, we were fond of him. *Bah!* that was his natural state to be like that ! A noble, you see——"

" Yet there must have been a catastrophe that caused the violent separation of Monsieur and Madame de Merret ?"

" I did not say that there had been a catastrophe, sir, I know of none."

" That's right. Now I am sure that you know all about it."

" Well, sir, I will tell you the truth. When I saw Monsieur Regnault go upstairs to you, I did think he would mention Madame de Merret to you because of the *Grande Bretêche*. That gave me the idea of consulting you, sir, whom I take for a sensible man and one not likely to betray a poor woman like myself, who have never done any harm to any one, and who yet am tormented by my conscience. Till now I have never ventured to unburden myself to the people of this country,—a set of gossips with tongues like knives. Besides, sir, I have never had a lodger who has stayed in my inn as long as yourself, and to whom I could tell the story of the fifteen thousand francs."

"My dear Dame Lepas," I replied, staying her flood of words, "if what you are about to confide to me is of a compromising nature, for all the world I would not be burdened with it."

"Don't be afraid," she said, interrupting me. "You'll see."

From this eagerness, I inferred that I was not the only person to whom my good landlady had communicated the secret of which I was to be the sole recipient, and I prepared to listen.

"Sir," she said, "when the Emperor sent the Spanish prisoners of war and others here, the government quartered on me a young Spaniard who had been sent to Vendôme on parole. Parole notwithstanding, he went out every day to show himself to the *sous-préfet*. He was a Spanish grandee! Nothing less! His name ended in *os* and *dia*, something like Burgos de Férédia. I have his name on my books; you can read it, if you like. Oh! but he was a handsome young man for a Spaniard, which they are all said to be ugly. He was only five feet and a few inches high, but he was well-grown; he had small hands that he took such care of; ah! you should have seen! He had as many brushes for his hands as a woman for her whole dressing apparatus! He had thick black hair, a fiery eye, his skin was rather bronzed, but I liked the look of it. He wore the finest linen I have ever seen on any one, although I have had princesses staying here, and, among others, General

Bertrand, the Duke and Duchess d'Abrantès, Monsieur Decazes and the King of Spain. He didn't eat much; but his manners were so polite, so amiable, that one could not owe him a grudge. Oh! I was very fond of him, although he didn't open his lips four times in the day, and it was impossible to keep up a conversation with him. For if you spoke to him, he did not answer. It was a fad, a mania with them all, I heard say. He read his breviary like a priest, he went to mass and to all the services regularly. Where did he sit? Two steps from the chapel of Madame de Merret. As he took his place there the first time he went to church, nobody suspected him of any intention in so doing. Besides he never raised his eyes from his prayer-book, poor young man! After that, sir, in the evening he would walk on the mountains, among the castle ruins. It was the poor man's only amusement, it reminded him of his country. They say that Spain is all mountains!

From the commencement of his imprisonment he stayed out late. I was anxious when I found that he did not come home before midnight; but we got accustomed to this fancy of his. He took the key of the door, and we left off sitting up for him. He lodged in a house of ours in the *Rue des Casernes*. After that, one of our stable-men told us that in the evening when he led the horses to the water, he thought he had seen the Spanish grandee swimming far down the river like a live fish. When he returned, I told him to take care of the rushes; he appeared vexed to have been seen in the water. At last, one day, or rather one morning, we did not find him in his room; he had not returned. After searching everywhere, I found some writing in the drawer of a table, where there were fifty gold pieces of Spain that are called doubloons and were worth about five thousand francs; and ten thousand francs' worth of diamonds in a small sealed box. The writing said, that in case he did not return, he left us the money and the diamonds, on condition of paying for masses to thank God for his escape, and for his salvation. In those days my husband had not been taken from me; he hastened to seek him everywhere.

"And now for the strange part of the story. He brought home the Spaniard's clothes, that he had discovered under a big stone, in a sort of pile-work by the river-side near the castle, nearly opposite to the *Grande Bretêche.* My husband had gone there so early that no one had seen him. After reading the letter, he burned the clothes, and according to Count Férédia's desire we declared that he had escaped. The *sous-préfet* sent all the *gendarmerie* in pursuit of him; but *brust!* they never caught him. Lepas believed that the Spaniard had drowned himself. I, sir, don't think so; I am more inclined to believe that he had something to do with the affair of Madame de Merret, seeing that Rosalie told me that the crucifix that her mistress thought so much of, that she had it buried with her, was of ebony and silver. Now in the beginning of his stay here, Monsieur de Férédia had one in ebony and silver, that I never saw him with later. Now, sir, don't you consider that I need have no scruples about the Spaniard's fifteen thousand francs, and that I have a right to them?"

"Certainly; but you haven't tried to question Rosalie?" I said.

"Oh, yes, indeed, sir; but to no purpose! The girl's like a wall. She knows something, but it is impossible to get her to talk."

After exchanging a few more words with me, my landlady left me a prey to vague and gloomy thoughts, to a romantic curiosity, and a religious terror not unlike the profound impression produced on us when by night, on entering a dark church, we perceive a faint light under high arches; a vague figure glides by—the rustle of a robe or cassock is heard, and we shudder.

Suddenly the *Grande Bretêche* and its tall weeds, its barred windows, its rusty ironwork, its closed doors, its deserted apartments, appeared like a fantastic apparition before me. I essayed to penetrate the mysterious dwelling, and to find the knot of its dark story,—the drama that had killed three persons. In my eyes, Rosalie became the most interesting person in Vendôme. As I studied her, I discovered the traces of secret care, despite the radiant health that shone in her plump countenance. There was in her the germ of remorse or hope; her attitude revealed a secret, like the attitude of a bigot who prays to excess, or of the infanticide who ever hears the last cry of her child. Yet her manners were rough and ingenuous—her silly smile was not that of a criminal, and could you but have seen the great kerchief that encompassed her portly bust, framed and laced in by a lilac and blue cotton gown, you would have dubbed her innocent.   No, I thought, I will not leave Vendôme without learning the history of the *Grande Bretêche*.   To gain my ends I will strike up a friendship with Rosalie, if needs be.

" Rosalie," said I, one evening.

" Sir ? "

" You are not married ? "

She started slightly.

" Oh, I can find plenty of men, when the fancy takes me to be made miserable," she said, laughing.

She soon recovered from the effects of her emotion, for all women, from the great lady to the maid of the inn, possess a composure that is peculiar to them.

" You are too good looking and well favoured to be short of lovers.   But tell me, Rosalie, why did you take service in an inn after leaving Madame de Merret ?   Did she leave you nothing to live on ? "

"Oh, yes! But, sir, my place is the best in all Vendôme."

This reply was one of those that judges and lawyers would call evasive. Rosalie appeared to me to be situated in this romantic history like the square in the midst of a chessboard. She was at the heart of the truth and chief interest; she seemed to me to be bound in the very knot of it. The conquest of Rosalie was no longer to be an ordinary siege,—in this girl was centred the last chapter of a novel; therefore from this moment Rosalie became the object of my preference.

By dint of studying the girl, I discovered endless good qualities in her, as one does in all women who become the chief objects of our thought. She was clean and tidy; she was handsome, of course; she soon acquired all the graces that our desire lends to women, in whatever grade they may happen to be.

One morning, a fortnight after the notary's visit, I said to Rosalie,—

"Tell me all you know about Madame de Merrot?"

"Oh!" she replied, in terror, "do not ask that of me, Monsieur Horace."

Her pretty face fell,—her clear bright colour faded,—and her eyes lost their innocent brightness.

"Well, then," she said at last, "if you must have it so, I will tell you about it; but promise to keep my secret!"

"*Va!* my dear girl, I must keep your secrets with the honour of a thief, which is the most loyal in the world."

"If it's the same to you," she said, "I prefer that it should be with your own." Thereupon she straightened her kerchief and assumed the attitude of a narrator,—for to be sure a confidential attitude and a certain security are requisite to the telling of a story. The best stories are told at a certain hour, at table, as we now are. No one has ever told a story well fasting or standing. But were I to transcribe Rosalie's diffuse eloquence faithfully, an entire volume would scarcely contain it. Now as the event she incoherently related to me, happens to be placed between the chatter of the notary and that of Madame Lepas, as exactly as the mean of a mathematical position between its two extremes, I can tell it you in a few words. So I shall abridge. The room occupied by Madame de Merret at the *Bretéche* was on the ground floor. A little closet about four feet deep, built in the thickness of the wall served as her wardrobe. Three months before the eventful evening of which I am about to speak, Madame de Merret had been so seriously indisposed that her husband had left her to herself in her own apartment, while he occupied another on the first floor. By one of those chances that it is impossible to foresee, he returned home from the club (where he was accustomed to read the papers and discuss politics with the inhabitants of the place) two hours later than usual. His wife supposed him to be at home, in bed and asleep. But the invasion of France had been the subject of a most animated discussion ; the billiard match had been exciting, he had lost forty francs, an enormous sum for Vendôme, where every one hoards, and where manners are restricted within the limits of a praiseworthy modesty, which perhaps is the source of the true happiness that no Parisian covets. For some time past Monsieur de Merret had been satisfied to ask Rosalie if his wife had gone to bed : and on her reply, which was always in the affirmative, had immediately gained his own room with the good temper engendered by habit and confidence. On entering his house, he took it into his head to go and tell his wife of his misadventure, perhaps by way of consolation. At dinner he had found Madame de Merret most coquettishly attired. On his way to the club it had occurred to him that his wife was restored to health, and that her convalescence had added to her beauty. He was, as husbands are wont to be, somewhat slow in making this discovery. Instead of calling Rosalie, who was occupied just then in watching the cook and coachman play a difficult hand at *brisque*,* Monsieur de Merret went to his wife's room by the light of a lantern that he deposited on the first step of the staircase. His unmistakable step resounded under the vaulted corridor. At the moment that the Count turned the handle of his wife's door he fancied he could hear the door of the closet I spoke of close; but when he entered, Madame de Merret was alone before the fireplace. The husband thought ingenuously that Rosalie was in the closet, yet a suspicion that jangled in his ear put him on his guard. He looked at his wife and saw in her eyes I know not what wild and hunted expression.

"You are very late," she said. Her habitually pure, sweet voice seemed changed to him.

Monsieur de Merret did not reply, for at that mo-

---

* A game of cards.

ment Rosalie entered. It was a thunderbolt for him. He strode about the room, passing from one window to the other, with mechanical motion and folded arms.

"Have you heard bad news, or are you unwell?" inquired his wife timidly, while Rosalie undressed her.

He kept silent.

"You can leave me," said Madame de Merret to her maid; "I will put my hair in curl papers myself."

From the expression of her husband's face she foresaw trouble, and wished to be alone with him. When Rosalie had gone, or was supposed to have gone (for she stayed in the corridor for a few minutes), Monsieur de Merret came and stood in front of his wife, and coldly said to her,—

"Madam, there is some one in your closet!" She looked calmly at her husband and replied simply,—

"No, sir."

This answer was heartrending to Monsieur de Merret; he did not believe in it. Yet his wife had never appeared to him purer or more saintly than at that moment. He rose to open the closet door; Madame de Merret took his hand, looked at him with an expression of melancholy, and said in a voice that betrayed singular emotion,—

"If you find no one there, remember this, all will be over between us!" The extraordinary dignity of his wife's manner restored the Count's profound esteem for her, and inspired him with one of those resolutions that only lack a vaster stage to become immortal.

"No," said he, "Josephine, I will not go there. in either case it would separate us for ever. Hear me, I know how pure you are at heart, and that your life is a holy one. You would not commit a mortal sin, to save your life."

At these words, Madame de Merret turned a haggard gaze upon her husband.

"Here, take your crucifix," he added. "Swear to me before God, that there is no one in there; I will believe you, I will never open that door."

Madame de Merret took the crucifix and said,—

"I swear."

"Louder," said the husband, "and repeat, 'I swear before God that there is no one in that closet.'" She repeated the sentence calmly.

"That will do," said Monsieur de Merret coolly. After a moment of silence,—

"I never saw this pretty toy before," he said, examining the ebony crucifix inlaid with silver, and most artistically chiselled.

"I found it at Duvivier's, who bought it of a Spanish monk when the prisoners passed through Vendôme last year."

"Ah!" said Monsieur de Merret as he replaced the crucifix on the nail, and he rang. Rosalie did not keep him waiting. Monsieur de Merret went quickly to meet her, led her to the bay window that opened on to the garden and whispered to her,—

"Listen! I know that Gorenflot wishes to marry you, poverty is the only drawback, and you told him that you would be his wife if he found the means to establish himself as a master mason. . . . Well! go and fetch him, tell him to come here with his trowel and his tools. Manage not to awaken any one in his house but himself; his fortune will be more than your desires. Above all, leave this room without babbling, otherwise . . ." He frowned. Rosalie went away, he recalled her.

"Here, take my latchkey," he said.

"Jean!" then cried Monsieur de Merret in tones of thunder in the corridor. Jean, who was at the same time his coachman and his confidential servant, left his game of cards and came.

"Go to bed, all of you," said his master, signing to him to approach; and the Count added under his breath: "When they are all asleep—*asleep, d'ye* hear? —you will come down and tell me." Monsieur de Merret, who had not lost sight of his wife, all the time he was giving his orders, returned quietly to her, at the fireside, and began to tell her the events of the game of billiards, and the talk of the club. When Rosalie returned, she found Monsieur and Madame de Merret conversing very amicably.

The Count had lately had all the ceilings of his reception rooms on the ground floor repaired. Plaster of Paris is difficult to obtain in Vendôme; the carriage raises its price. The Count had therefore bought a good deal, being well aware that he could find plenty of .purchasers for whatever might remain over. This circumstance inspired him with the design he was about to execute.

"Sir, Gorenflot has arrived," said Rosalie in low tones.

"Show him in," replied the Count in loud tones.

Madame de Merret turned rather pale when she saw the mason.

"Gorenflot," said her husband, "go and fetch bricks from the coachhouse, and bring sufficient to wall up the door of this closet; you will use the plaster I have over to coat the wall with." Then, calling Rosalie and the workman aside,—

"Listen, Gorenflot," said he in an undertone; "you will sleep here to-night. But to-morrow you will have a passport to a foreign country, to a town to which I will direct you. I shall give you six thousand francs for your journey. You will stay ten years in that town; if you did not like it, you might establish yourself in another, providing it be in the same country. You will pass through Paris, where you will await me. There I will insure you an additional six thousand francs by contract, which will be paid you on your return, providing you have fulfilled the conditions of our bargain. This is the price for your absolute silence as to what you are about to do to-night. As to you, Rosalie, I will give you ten thousand francs on the day of your wedding, on condition of your marrying Gorenflot; but if you wish to marry, you must hold your tongues; or,—no dowry."

"Rosalie," said Madame de Merret, "do my hair."

The husband walked calmly up and down, watching the door, the mason and his wife, but without betraying any insulting doubts. Madame de Merret chose a moment when the workman was unloading bricks and her husband was at the other end of the room, to say to Rosalie: "A thousand francs a year for you, my child, if you can tell Gorenflot to leave a chink at the bottom." Then out loud, she added coolly,—

"Go and help him!"

Monsieur and Madame de Merret were silent all the time that Gorenflot took to brick up the door. This silence, on the part of the husband, who did not choose to furnish his wife with a pretext for saying things of a double meaning, had its purpose; on the part of Madame de Merret it was either pride or prudence. When the wall was about half way up, the sly workman took advantage of a moment when the Count's back was turned, to strike a blow with his trowel in one of the glass panes of the closet-door. This act informed Madame de Merret that Rosalie had spoken to Gorenflot.

All three then saw a man's face, it was dark and gloomy with black hair and eyes of flame. Before her husband turned, the poor woman had time to make a sign to the stranger that signified: Hope!

At four o'clock, towards dawn, for it was the month of September, the construction was finished. The mason was handed over to the care of Jean, and Monsieur de Merret went to bed in his wife's room.

On rising the following morning he said carelessly,—

"The deuce! I must go to the *Mairie* for the

passport. He put his hat on his head, advanced three steps towards the door, altered his mind, and took the crucifix.

His wife trembled for joy. "He is going to Duvivier," she thought. As soon as the Count had left Madame de Merret rang for Rosalie; then in a terrible voice,—

"The trowel, the trowel," she cried, "and quick to work! I saw how Gorenflot did it; we shall have time to make a hole and to mend it again."

In the twinkling of an eye Rosalie brought a sort of mattock to her mistress, who with unparalleled ardour set about demolishing the wall. She had already knocked out several bricks, and was preparing herself to strike a more decisive blow, when she perceived Monsieur de Merret behind her. She fainted.

"Lay Madame on her bed," said the Count coolly. He had foreseen what would happen in his absence, and had set a trap for his wife; he had simply written to the mayor, and had sent for Duvivier. The jeweller arrived just as the room had been put in order.

"Duvivier," inquired the Count, "did you buy crucifixes of the Spaniards who passed through here?"

"No, sir."

"That will do, thank you," he said, looking at his wife like a tiger. "Jean," he added, "you will see that my meals are served in the Countess's room; she is ill, and I shall not leave her until she has recovered."

The cruel gentleman stayed with his wife for twenty days. In the beginning, when there were sounds in the walled closet, and Josephine attempted to implore his pity for the dying stranger, he replied, without permitting her to say a word,—

"You have sworn on the cross that there is no one there."

After this story, all the ladies rose from table and

the spell cast over them by the Doctor * was broken by this movement. Yet some of them nearly felt a cold shiver while they listened to his last words.

* The *Bianchon* of the *Scènes de la Vie Privée.*

Butler & Tanner, The Selwood Printing Works, Frome, and London.